the w

D0242976

007059108 3

Also by Lucy Worsley

Eliza Rose

My Name is Victoria

LADY MARY

LUCY WORSLEY

Illustrated by Joe Berger

BLOOMSBURY
CHILDREN'S BOOKS

LONDON   OXFORD   NEW YORK   NEW DELHI   SYDNEY

BLOOMSBURY CHILDREN'S BOOKS
Bloomsbury Publishing Plc
50 Bedford Square, London, WC1B 3DP, UK

BLOOMSBURY, BLOOMSBURY CHILDREN'S BOOKS
and the Diana logo are trademarks of Bloomsbury Publishing Plc

First published in Great Britain in 2018 by Bloomsbury Publishing Plc

A catalogue record for this book is available from the British Library

ISBN: PB: 978-1-4088-6944-4; eBook: 978-1-4088-7013-6

2 4 6 8 10 9 7 5 3 1

Typeset by RefineCatch Limited, Bungay, Suffolk

Printed and bound in Great Britain by CPI Group (UK) Ltd, Croydon CR0 4YY

MIX
Paper from
responsible sources
FSC® C020471

To find out more about our authors and books visit www.bloomsbury.com
and sign up for our newsletters

To Emma Hindley,
with thanks for all
the Tudor fun

Contents

Part Two: In Exile

Part Three: Return to Court

Prologue

April 1525, Greenwich,

in the Queen's Bedchamber, Mary is nine …

'Press a little harder with the pen, Mary. Your letters are all faint.'

'Like a spider's footsteps.'

Mary had spoken without thinking, but the image was striking, and it made her mother laugh. The tiny feet of a spider, trailing across the paper. Yes, Mary's handwriting was difficult to read, unlike the bold, strong strokes of her mother's draft that she was copying.

'Mary! You are daydreaming again, aren't you?'

'Yes, *Mother*. Daydreaming. As always.'

'No need to be pert!'

Mary returned her attention to the task, but the spider wouldn't leave her mind. She imagined him stopping a moment for a sit-down, crossing his many legs. It made her giggle. Laboriously, she tried to copy out the next few words.

… my heart and soul will always be yours …

Her mother was hovering anxiously, and Mary wished she would go away. Mary did not mind writing, even enjoyed it sometimes, but she hated to be watched. Yet she had to do this for Charles, the emperor, her beloved. Yes, he was her beloved. She had been told it so many times that she almost believed it. Mary stroked her gold brooch, its letters spelling out his name: THE EMPEROUR.

Mary's mother noticed what she was doing.

'Ah yes!' she said, delighted. 'You are thinking of your husband-to-be. I see it! Thoughts of love and honour fill your head, *angelito mio*. What a magnificent future you have ahead of you – an empress! Nothing could be better, nothing more splendid. Your Spanish grandmother would be proud.'

Mary was so used to her mother's rhapsodies about her imperial future that she barely listened. But while her ears might not have been working, her eyes certainly were.

'What's that, Mother?'

Mary noticed that Queen Catherine was holding something in her own fingers, turning it over and over, as if it were precious. She looked up from her examination of the tiny, glinting object, a triumphant smile on her face.

'Can you see what it is?'

Mary peered. It was a ring, clearly. But what kind?

Mary racked her brains for the colours of the precious stones that she had learned with Mr Featherstone. What colour was it? She examined it, turning it to the light.

'It's green, isn't it? Is it … an emerald?'

'Yes!' Her mother was rapturous, in a way that always slightly embarrassed Mary. It was easy to learn her lessons from Mr Featherstone. It was harder to know what to say in any given situation. She wished, often, for less fuss and to be left alone with her thoughts. Mary rolled her eyes. Green and gold, green and gold; they were her mother's favourite colours.

'It's a huge emerald, isn't it?' her mother continued. 'As green as poison. And in a magnificent setting of gold as well. This will be your gift to your *amado*, Mary. We will send it with your letter.'

Mary slightly lost interest in the ring, if it was to pass so quickly through her possession. 'Oh Mary,' her mother sighed. 'You are not like other girls. You aren't interested in jewels, are you? Don't you want to keep it for yourself?'

'Not really,' Mary admitted. 'I would rather have a sister. Or, if I can't have a sister, then a kitten.' Mary knew that she shouldn't ask for a sister, or a baby brother. It made her mother upset. 'Yes, I'd rather have a kitten,' she said definitively.

Her ruse worked. 'Oh no, not kittens again!' The queen was exasperated. 'They have fleas, *querida*. And there is no place for them in the train of an army.'

'But Mother!' This time Mary's attention was captured to the extent that she threw down her pen. 'I am not in the train of an army. I will never be in the train of an army. I am stuck here in this royal palace, with nothing much to do, and nobody to play with, and loads of people gawping at me whenever I set foot out of our chamber.'

Catherine at once looked very grim, and crouched down by Mary's chair, looking sternly into her daughter's face.

'You,' she said savagely, holding Mary's eyes and jabbing at Mary's chest with her finger, 'are a daughter of Spain. You will not always be kept safe inside this *luxurious* palace, as you are now. You will look back on this as a time of great good fortune. The Wheel of Fortune can take you down as well as up, you know.'

'But *Mother*,' Mary said drily. She tired of this debate. She crossed her arms, sulky again. 'My father is the king of England. Who could know better than him? And he says that women don't go to war.' It really was too exhausting to have this argument over and over again.

Catherine continued exactly as if Mary had not spoken. 'The time will come for bravery,' she said, tapping a finger on the table. 'You are a daughter of Spain,' she said. 'Your grandmother Isabella was a warrior queen. Even when with child she rode to war! And daughters of Spain are always ready to fight! To fight to the death!'

Mary sighed. 'But I don't want to fight to the death,' she said under her breath. 'We're not in the country of the blood-drinkers now.'

She had heard her father refer to Spain in this manner. Although she did not know if Spaniards really did drink blood – what, out of goblets? – she thought it sounded impressively dismissive. But her mother wasn't listening.

'When you are married to Charles …'

Catherine was clicking her fingers to regain Mary's attention. It worked. Mary turned to find her mother's blue eyes blazing at her, a sharp crease between her eyebrows.

'When you are married to Charles, when you have come of age in a few years' time, you will be an empress. You will have many enemies. People will try to take your power away from you. You must always, *always* be ready to fight to the death. I give you a great gift in telling you this.'

Mary's attention wandered again, as it so often did. She tried to imagine being married to Charles. She had of course met him, four years ago, when their marriage contract had been drawn up. But it would still be another four years until she would go to Brussels and live with him. It was hard to remember his face. It was hard to imagine being an empress, and being ready to fight to the death every single day.

'I'd rather be queen of England than an empress,' Mary said, with decision. 'Can't Charles come and live with me here?' What a lovely thought this was! 'He could live here, with me, and you, and Father!' Mary spun round to her mother, stretching out her arms in enthusiasm, the letter forgotten, enraptured with her new idea.

Catherine's fierce look dissipated in an instant, as it often did when something amused her. But then a shadow crossed her face. She turned back to Mary, revealing her profile like a hawk's, her heavy eyelids that came down half over her pupils, making her look ancient, timeless.

'Girls like you, *Princess* Mary,' Mary's mother said, 'must always go to live abroad. Like I did, you know that! And you should be pleased to leave this miserable land of England, where they don't care for girls anyway. Just look at the way your father insists that he still has no children. No children! Despite having you, a wondrous Spanish beauty. Although you have red-gold hair – that's not so Spanish. But of course you get that from me.'

Mary lowered her chin to her chest. Red-gold hair, *indeed*. It was more like a sort of warm light brown. And despite her mother's pride in the colour of Mary's hair, she personally thought it was the same shade as her father's. It was kind of her mother to call her a beauty, but Mary was suspicious of such terms. She had often examined her nose in the curve of the silver water jug. It flared, rather like the nose of a mule. She would turn her head from side to side, trying to make it look smaller, and indeed, at a certain point the swell of the vessel would make it disappear. All bad things could disappear, she thought, if you looked at them in the right light. But what was it that her mother was going on about now? The letter, oh, the letter. Yes, she must finish the letter to Charles.

The half-empty page looked enormous. Mary's writing had so far only filled a tiny bit at the top. She should have started lower down, so as to make it look like a long letter with less work. She picked up her pen.

Will anything even come of it? Mary asked herself as she dipped it into the ink. Charles never wrote back. Mary sometimes suspected that her mother *went on* about things too much, and that this had the effect of boring people and turning them away. Too many letters; too many words.

She tried to imagine Charles reading the letter, trying on the ring. But what came to mind was a frowning man tossing the letter aside, as her father so often did. Secretaries picked up his discarded correspondence afterwards, from the floor, and took it away to deal with it, while he instead strode out saying that he was going hunting.

'Perhaps,' she said tentatively, 'I write too often to Charles. Perhaps it bores him to receive all these letters.'

'Mary! It is *your duty* to write often to your *amado*.'

It wasn't easy to suggest that her mother might ever be wrong.

Mary sighed. She had known, really, that she would not get off so easily. 'He needs to be reminded,'

Catherine said, as if to herself, 'of his ties to Spain. Of his ties to me, his aunt, stuck here in this damp island and married to a piece of soft curds of cheese. He needs reminding,' she said, her voice rising, 'of his own duty, which is *to marry my daughter*.'

'Soft curds?' In her mother's ravings, these were the only words that Mary picked out. 'My father is not *soft like cheese*, you know!'

'Ah, you are indignant, my spitting cat!' Catherine said, with a laugh. 'That's the spirit. I never knew such a girl for daydreaming, nor one who more admired her father. You worship him too much. You should save your worship for God!'

'Honour thy father and mother,' Mary said primly. 'Isn't that true?'

Catherine knelt again, looking closely into Mary's face. For a moment Mary feared that she'd get told off for answering back.

But not this time.

'It *is* true,' Catherine said gently. 'But *especially* honour your mother, and honour God. That is the Spanish way. There are many spies and liars in the world, but you must always, always trust me.

Now, to work. Finish writing out that letter and then we can play.'

I *would prefer to make up my own letter rather than copy yours*, Mary thought to herself rebelliously as she pulled the draft closer to see it better. *And my father is not soft like cheese at all. He says that girls can't be king. And because he's the king, and knows everything in the world, he can't be wrong.*

PART ONE

AT COURT

Chapter 1

April 1527, Greenwich

Mary is eleven ...

'And where ...'

The great bellowing roar came from the courtyard outside the window. Mary looked up, delighted.

'And where is the high ...'

The deep, booming voice was louder now, coming closer, climbing the stairs. Mary had been stuck in a velvet chair for hours, with her mother's ladies fussing all around her, doing her hair and fastening heavy necklaces around her throat until her head almost ached with the strain of remaining upright. She felt the gold links move and clank a little as she stretched her neck round to look between the ladies towards the door.

'And where is the high, mighty and powerful princess ...'

Mary was now giggling, and wiggling out of her chair, and darting between the ladies-in-waiting. It was two years later. Mary knew that she was too grown up, now, for playing the old games with her father. But somehow, she could not stop. Behind her, she sensed her mother's body give a slight resigned droop, and her unwilling smile.

'The PRINCESS MARY?'

With that, Mary's father was in the queen's bedchamber, and picking Mary up under the arm-pits, and spinning her round and round in the air. She shrieked with excitement.

'Oof!'

Unceremoniously, her father dumped her to the floor. The ladies-in-waiting did their usual trick of disappearing, slipping away silently with serene smiles. As they left, they revealed Mary's mother standing by the dressing table.

'Yes,' said Catherine drily. 'She is not so light now that she is eleven!'

'Eleven, nearly a lady! And nearly ready to be

married! Now, let me see you.'

Mary's father had been staggering about, pretending that she had broken his back, while she smirked and giggled. But now he drew himself up and settled his fur-trimmed robe back on his shoulders.

'Come on, stand up straight!' Mary's father said, scanning her up and down with his blue eyes. 'Let us see this princess of ours! The ambassadors are here from your suitor, and they want to inspect you. They'll report back to him, you know.'

'Oh, I think that our daughter will make you proud,' said Catherine lightly. She stepped forward and placed her hands on Mary's shoulders. 'Stand straight, *angelito mio*,' she whispered in Mary's ear.

Mary slowly twirled for her father in her velvet dress and necklaces, slightly resisting the pressure of her mother's hands.

'Have we not done well, my love?'

Queen Catherine showed off two hours' handi-work in Mary's carefully selected velvet gown. She and her ladies had sewn Mary into it, stitching pearls along her neckline and braiding her hair into a crown. Although she was eleven, Mary was too young, still, to hide her hair under a pointed hat like her mother's. She sometimes longed to feel the weight of such a headdress. Then she would be grown up, and probably married. People would take her seriously, not just tell her how clever she was, then move the conversation on to other things.

'Where are her fur-trimmed sleeves?'

He was asking suspiciously.

Catherine pantomimed surprise.

'I thought she was to play the virginals,' she said.

'Catherine, don't start again. This is all agreed. Yes, my daughter is certainly to play the virginals.'

Mary twitched at the sudden chill in the atmosphere. She knew that it had been long ago confirmed that she would perform for the ambassadors on the virginals, despite her mother's reluctance to have her do so.

'It *is* agreed, my liege,' Catherine said, smooth as silk. She was using a voice that Mary thought of as treacherous. She would say the nicest things in this voice, but she didn't mean them. 'Oh yes, it *is* agreed that Princess Mary will play the virginals. And for that she cannot wear her heavy sleeves. That's why she is not wearing them, obviously.

They're quite safe, here in the box.' She nodded to a heavy leather trunk, brought up that morning from the royal wardrobe department in London, and raided by the ladies for Mary's costume.

Catherine's father nodded, appeased.

'All right, no sleeves,' he said. 'I'll give you credit, Catherine – you might not want this match for our daughter, but you have made her look as fine as any princess in Europe.'

Mary was not feeling particularly fine. In fact, she was beginning to feel more than a little foolish under her heavy clothes and her parents' scrutiny. Her scalp was starting to complain where her hair had been plaited a bit too tight. But then, her father's approval was important. He so rarely came up to see them in their chamber. It was worth going through all this to make him proud.

'Up, stand up straight!' he said tetchily. 'And what's this? Oh, but this is a nice touch.'

Mary pressed out her chest, where she was wearing a golden brooch.

'THE DUKE, it says,' she told him proudly. 'My one true love.'

For a second she felt her parents' eyes meeting over her head, and something powerful being exchanged. She felt cross. It was always like this. She was called the first princess of Europe, and then the next second she was utterly ignored. Much better to be an animal, she decided. Life as a princess was rather like being a piece of fine furniture, to be admired, cooed over, then swiftly forgotten.

'Yes,' said Catherine. 'Mary's heart is committed to this French duke now. The brooch makes it plain who owns her: the French people. I had hoped that she would marry my nephew, the emperor. I admit it. I had hoped that she would not be called upon to play the virginals once more, to yet another set of ambassadors, like a common wench on display, to be sold to the highest bidder. I had hoped to avoid that for *our daughter, the princess*. But I have embraced it in good faith.'

Mary's fingers felt the outline of her brooch once more. THE DUKE, it read, in golden letters, meaning the younger son of the king of France. She didn't mind, really, that her betrothed was no longer Charles, the emperor, but Henri, the Duke d'Orléans. And THE DUKE was no easier to imagine than THE EMPEROUR, although her mother was much less keen on him.

Henry smiled. 'I understand your dislike of the French,' he said. 'No one can fault you, Catherine, on your constancy. Nor your devotion to that fierce old-fashioned God of yours. But today let's be merry. Have we not got a fine girl? The ambassadors will love her. And how your fingers twinkle on those keys, hey, Mary? You get your musical skills from your father.'

He was taking her hand again, and now spinning her round into a dance, drawing Catherine reluctantly into the movement. '*C'est bonjour, monsieur*,' he sang, to a silly tune of his own devising, 'this prince, this *duc d'Orléans*, he will be your husband, Mary! And maybe one day you'll be queen of France, which is second only to being queen of England.'

At that, he bowed down with a sweeping gesture towards his wife. Of course, Mary's mother really was queen of England. Despite her constant talk of Spain, which made Mary forget it from time to time.

Catherine extricated herself with dignity, but her husband's buffoonery caused an unwilling smile to creep across her face. As Mary continued to join her father in his ridiculous capering, she craned her neck to watch her mother, anxious to see her happy. Mary could see that the crease between Catherine's eyes had not disappeared. But she did manage to give Mary a tight little grin.

Soothed, Mary stopped dancing, and placed her hand formally in her father's.

'I'm ready,' she said. 'Take me to my *amado*.'

'Your *bien-aimé*,' her father corrected her.

They both sensed Catherine's small angry gesture behind them at his use of French rather than Spanish. The king stopped suddenly in the doorway, forcing Mary to stop too.

'You are not a princess of Spain now, *Catherine*,' he said sternly. 'It's no part of your duty to hate the French as the Spanish do. You are a queen of England, and my wife, and I say it is your duty to love the French. And I hope you will come down to the party tonight, to see our daughter dance with the French ambassador. I don't want any talk of your being ill, and I don't want you skulking away and eating your dinner up here in your room.'

'Oh, I'll be there,' said Catherine coldly. 'But it's been three suitors for our daughter now, and she's only eleven. First the dauphin; then the emperor; now this Duke of Orléans. To whom will you marry our daughter off next? You are fickle, my love, fickle like the wind.'

Mary knew that her father had a burning desire to answer. He expressed it through the savage squeeze he gave to her hand. She knew that he was struggling with himself, for one second, for two. But he did manage to remain silent. He pulled Mary with him through the door.

'Spaniards!' he muttered as they went down the stairs. 'Blood-drinkers! What a bloody stubborn race they are.'

Chapter 2

April 1527, Greenwich

Later, much later, the same day, Mary was sleepy. It was past her usual bedtime. The green gown had grown extremely heavy and was hurting where it hung from her hips. As she walked with her mother through the palace, Mary began to shuffle and stumble with her feet. She trod on the hem of her long skirt.

Catherine noticed, and grabbed Mary's hand to force her to keep up. 'Hold your dress up properly, Mary,' she hissed. 'Use your other hand.' It was a chilly evening, a wet wind had been blowing in across the river, and the air was damp and cold from the rain even now falling hard upon the roof.

'Mother, I've had about enough of celebrating,'

Mary said. 'Can't I go to bed?' Both hands were trapped now, and she felt like a prisoner.

'No, you can't,' said Catherine grimly. 'Court celebrations aren't for fun, you know. They're work. They're your job as a princess, and mine as a queen. And you must look like you are happy and proud to be present. That is the secret of success.'

Not for fun. All too often Mary had heard those words. She hung her head, dispirited. Her mother noticed, and relented a little.

'Courage!' Queen Catherine said. 'Just one more hour to go. Then you can go to bed. You played well today. Don't you ever get nervous?'

'A daughter of Spain never feels pain,' chanted Mary, something her mother often said, even though it wasn't true. She would have liked to close her eyes there and then, as keeping them open almost hurt. In fact, she did close them, pretending for a minute that she was sleepwalking.

'Ah, you have a gift, Mary,' the queen said, laughing softly. 'You can lose yourself in music, can you not? And reading? You can live inside yourself. That is important for a princess. You will be much alone.'

Mary opened her eyes long enough to consider the question. She *felt* like she was never alone, never left to play, or think, or just to lie around doing nothing.

But yes, when she was playing her music, she did not notice the people around her. She *had* felt nervous when she entered the Great Chamber, it was true, for there were many people there, more people than she could remember seeing at court before. Then, though, she had seen the table laid with a carpet, and upon it the little square box of her instrument. Seating herself, she had simply pushed up her linen cuffs and played. It seemed to have worked.

Afterwards there had been a great deal of talk between her father and the ambassadorial party from France, and inevitably the focus moved off from Mary. Most of the talk had seemed to consist of technical and boring descriptions of the staffing of the court of the French king, punctuated by Mary's father's great booming laugh. Come to think of it, she did not remember her mother speaking once the whole afternoon. She had just sat there, a mysterious smile on her face, like a basilisk.

And there was something a little grim in the grip of her mother's hand dragging her along the corridor now.

'*Can't* we go to bed?' Mary asked, hearing a whimpering tone that she disliked in her voice. It only came out when she was tired, or hungry, but she felt unable to control it.

'No, we cannot,' said her mother. 'It is the will of your father that we should be present, and our absence will be noticed. Also, you want to show off your green dress, do you not? We're on duty!'

Mary did not think her dress particularly pretty – it was a stiff green brocade with a pattern of golden flowers woven in – but she looked down at it and straightened her brooch. The brooch had been a very good idea of her mother's. When the French ambassador had seen it, he'd burst into delighted laughter and bowed very low. But Mary would have preferred to wear something lighter and floatier, something, oh, something in a brighter colour than her mother's favourite – and endless – green.

As they turned the corner of the gallery, Mary started to hear the faint strain of music, the high piping notes of an oboe. The sound, a teasing tune, lifted her spirits. Suddenly she began to feel more awake. Her mother noticed. 'Ah yes,' she said. 'It is true that the English court can put on a good show, even in this miserable endless rain. Now, *Princess* Mary, remember you *are* a princess, and dance with dignity.'

They picked up their pace, and moved along the gallery towards the Great Hall.

It was warmer now, and the air seemed richer, even perfumed. The entryway was thronged with people. Mary was not surprised when they turned towards her mother, exclaimed, bowed and parted to let them through. This was the way it was at the palace of Greenwich. She and her mother never had to wait for anything. And if they did, why then her mother would lose her temper. Everyone was afraid of that, and did all they could to avoid it. Mary knew that even her father feared one of her mother's explosions.

Mary nodded to the bent heads and lifted hats, suddenly feeling alive, and curious as to what might lie beyond. As they entered, she saw that the hall was lined on each side with crowds of courtiers, mainly men, but several women too. A great blast of heat came out from the burning braziers and the people and the candles. Mary's eye dwelt particularly on the unfamiliar women among the crowd, in their beautiful, bright dresses. One lady had curiously highly arched eyebrows, so curved that they almost looked like they weren't real but drawn on with a pencil. Another had hair in tiny, perfect curls like the whorls of a snail.

She wanted to look for longer at the French ladies, but the French ambassador, whom she recognised from the afternoon, was bowing down before her and offering her his hand for a dance. Mary panicked for a moment. What was the correct response? Did she even know this dance? But then she felt her mother give a little shove in the small of her back. A daughter of Spain never feels pain, her mother always said. Mary paused to gather herself, swaying ever so slightly on her feet, remembering for half an instant how tired she was before taking his hand.

It was a relief, seconds later, when the music started again. Oh yes, of course she knew this dance;

it was a pavane. After a stately curtsey, she promenaded alongside the French gentleman, noticing that he had a small, sharp, clipped beard, which he nodded in time to the music. It made him look rather like her mother's cockatoo bird; oh yes, he had just the same chin whiskers.

Mary kept her eyes firmly fixed on her partner's funny little beard, because now she sensed that the whole room was looking at them. It was important not to make a mess of this. She tried to blot out the crowd and concentrate, giving all her attention to prancing in a stately manner down the room and bowing solemnly to the other couples left and right. This was how her mother had told her to get through, by concentrating on doing the right thing, one step at a time. Mary sometimes wondered if there was any more to it than this. Maybe there wasn't, in which case Mary might change her mind, she thought, and not be a princess after all.

But there was one person she couldn't ignore. He must be here, although she hadn't seen him yet. Where was her father? Oh, there he was. He was bowing to her, just as if she were a real grown-up lady, and he was twinkling at her with his blue eyes. What blue eyes they were, Mary thought, not a dull grey like her own. Her father's clear, bright blue ones must be the handsomest eyes at court. The lady with him clearly thought so, too, for she was so busy looking up at him that she completely failed to notice and to bow to Mary as all the other dancers had done.

But then Mary saw that she was one of the French ladies, and didn't know who Mary was. On her return up the hall, though, the lady again failed to bow, and this time Mary realised that she had seen that disrespectful face before. It was one of her own mother's ladies-in-waiting, the one that her mother didn't like, Mistress Anne Boleyn. Catherine was always giving Mistress Boleyn the afternoon off, not through kindness, but because she didn't want to have her around. Of course Mary recognised Mistress Boleyn now – it had just been the violet gown that had made Mary think her French.

But her father seemed quite happy. Watching him dancing with the snail-haired Mistress Boleyn, Mary lost her footing for a moment. There was a gasp from the nearest dancers. Of course they had noticed. Seething, Mary regained her balance, wishing that a tiny misstep did not always have to be made into such a drama. Her partner, seeing something of her feelings, grasped her hand more tightly, and smiled. Mary tried to smile back, recognising that his intentions were good. But then her eyes travelled past him, to her mother, who was not dancing. She was standing still as a statue, watching the ball around her and looking as cold as ice.

Mary sighed. Why could her mother never be happy? She was at least supposed to look like she was happy, wasn't she? Something of Mary's earlier weariness returned. The room no longer seemed rich and glamorous but hot and distressing. She stumbled again, and her partner took her arm and led her out from among the dancers.

'The princess is weary,' he said, 'and no surprise, it is very late. Please sit, please rest, and perhaps I may tell you of your future life in France?' She agreed, sitting down on the splendid velvet chair on the dais and gesturing him to sit on the stool beside her as she had seen her mother do to favoured visitors.

The dancers started up again, and Mary noticed with relief that the attention of the spectators returned to the centre of the hall.

'This palace of Greenwich is very fine,' he began, 'and in France too you will see many magnificent palaces.' He began to enumerate them, one by one, but they all sounded rather similar to each other. Mary began to feel her eyelids growing heavy, and as the dance wore on, she caught her head lolling to one side and had to jerk it upright.

Then her mother was before her. 'The princess is tired,' she said crisply, holding out one hand.

'But Your Majesty has not yet danced with the king!' cried the cockatoo gentleman, raising his hands as if to keep her at the ball.

'I will not be dancing tonight.'

At that precise moment, the dancers parted, and Mary saw that her father was still holding hands with the violet-gowned lady. In fact, he was holding both of her hands, and he was holding them closely too, cradling one of her elbows with his big clumsy paw. Mary knew what that felt like, for he loved to toss her up in the air, or to dance with her himself.

The Frenchman bowed silently, and silently Mary got to her feet and followed her mother out of the room. The ball had been very strange. The day had been very strange. Everyone had been so polite, so cordial, so appreciative, but there was something not quite right.

Chapter 3

April 1527, Greenwich

'Ah! The Princess Mary is here.'

It seemed a long way across the matting of the privy chamber. It was the morning after, and Mary had found it difficult to wake up. She had rolled over and gone back to sleep twice before her mother had come back to their bed and turfed her out.

Now her father was seated on his throne under its velvet canopy, and all around him the court and the French party were assembled. Before the dais was a table and two secretaries, taking notes upon great pages of parchment. Mary wondered why there were two. One she recognised, she had seen him before, but then she noticed that the other had that sunburned, moustachioed French look. He must work for the French king, keeping his own record of the discussion.

Mary nodded back to the ladies-in-waiting who had followed her in. Silently, smoothly, they peeled off from her wake to line the walls. She knew that her mother prided herself on the efficiency of their ladies-in-waiting, and Mary knew that they had done their job exactly right. Her father would notice – he noticed such things – and be pleased. Among the ladies was Mary's special friend Nan, Lady Hussey, who gave Mary the very tiniest quarter-wink. It raised her spirits at exactly the right moment.

Steeling herself, Mary trudged forward. No, this was wrong, she must glide, glide, into the centre of the room, and when she arrived she must curtsey. Once she was down low, she raised her eyes to give a secret smile to her father, and he smiled back. He gestured to a stool. Under the eyes of so many people, it was hard to sit down on a stool without wobbling. But eventually Mary got herself positioned by her father's knee, and the room's attention moved on. Phew, it was over, at least for now.

'Alors, where were we?'

It was the French ambassador himself, who now gave Mary a beam. She remembered that she had fallen asleep last night while he was talking to her, and she suddenly felt ashamed. That was not an action worthy of a princess. Although, she told herself, he really had been very boring.

'We have covered the household, the dowry … issues of religion,' said her father's secretary, looking down at the notes before him. Mary silently wondered just how long this would last. She always rather dreaded being called into the privy chamber because there was no knowing how long she would have to sit there, watching and listening to men saying things that she didn't understand. Today she had looked forward to it a little more, for she knew that the topic was to be her own marriage settlement.

There was a whispering. The French secretary, half standing, had his hand near the ear of the French ambassador, and was conveying information in a hiss.

'Ah yes.' The French ambassador spoke again.

'Now we have a further question, Your Majesty. It is to do with the issues of religion you mention. It has come to our master's attention, Your Majesty, that the princess's mother, the Princess Catalina of Spain, was married previously. That was before she made her second marriage to you after the death of your elder brother, of revered memory.'

Mary felt her father stir uneasily on the throne behind him.

'Well, what of it?'

There was a testy note in his voice. She thought that the ambassador would have been wiser not to ask this question about ancient history. She was well acquainted with the warning signs that lined the route towards her father's wrath.

'Excuse me!' The Frenchman was bowing ridiculously low. He must have been aware that he had given offence, and was trying to atone for it by abasing himself, practically to the matting. He had done well, but then, Mary thought, he must be familiar with the ways of kings. Sometimes the servants who brought in food and drink could not tell when the king was in a bad mood, and departed in comical haste if one of his explosions took them unawares.

Now the ambassador's nose was so near the floor that Mary almost had to stifle a giggle. It looked like he might never be able to get up again. Once more her father gave her a sidelong glance. Yes, they were both enjoying this. She distinctly heard a sharp report from the joint of the ambassador's bended knee, and saw him wince a little. But, despite his position, the ambassador didn't give up.

'It is well known,' the Frenchman continued, face still floorwards, 'that Your Majesty obtained a dispensation from the law of the Church when you married your wife. Because she had previously been married to your elder brother, and as we all know, the Pope has to give special permission for two brothers to marry the same bride.'

Mary frowned, wondering what he was talking about. She knew that she'd had an uncle, older than her father, and that her mother was supposed to have married him and had children with him, but that he'd died. Even her father, who seemed so utterly king-like and powerful, hadn't expected to become one. It was all down to the death of his brother, whose name was Arthur, when they had been very young.

'Yes, yes,' Henry said. 'We did get an exemption. Not that we needed one, you're wrong about that. But I'm pretty sure we got one to be on the safe side. Cardinal Wolsey will have the paperwork if your master really needs to see it.'

He was offhand now, speaking as if it hardly mattered. But Mary detected a note of strain in his voice, almost as if her father were bluffing.

The French ambassador's other knee cracked as he bowed again on the other leg, the better to address the rush matting anew. This time it didn't seem funny.

'It has come to our attention,' he said softly, 'that this dispensation was perhaps not valid. And that perhaps, therefore, your marriage was not valid, which would make this lovely young lady –' he nodded at Mary – 'erm, illegitimate, you know. You'll understand that these difficult questions must be addressed.'

'What can you mean?' Mary's father was on his

feet, roaring in outrage. 'How dare you! What evidence have you for this outrageous claim? What nonsense!'

Flustered, the ambassador was on his feet too, quite unable to continue bowing in the face of so much regal wrath. Mary tried to follow what was going on. Had he just suggested that she was illegitimate? The cheek! She tried to look affronted, but perhaps just succeeded in looking like she had toothache. She was eager to see what would happen next, how her father would eat up this impertinent man for breakfast.

But the Frenchman appeared – amazingly – to have more to say.

'Well, Your Majesty,' he said slowly. 'There is the matter of your offspring. If your marriage were approved by God, then surely you and the queen would have a male heir by now too? As well as this delightful young lady.' At that he cast a sideways look at Mary, half smiling, as if to indicate that he knew he was being indelicate but didn't wish to offend his dancing partner.

Mary pondered. It was true that she had no

brother. It was true that she had often heard her mother and father wishing that she did. Indeed, she would have liked to have had a brother or a sister herself. It would be fun to play with someone else, and, when her parents were in an arguing mood, there'd be someone else for them to argue over.

But then she shook herself and sat up straighter. The whole idea that God had deliberately denied her a brother was quite ridiculous.

'Oh, fiddlesticks!'

She did not realise that she'd spoken aloud. Everyone was looking at her, in some astonishment. Too late, she realised they were all waiting for her to continue. Perhaps she had better not have said anything, but this was so simple that it was easier, really, for her to put the ambassador right, rather than put her father to the trouble.

'Of course my father and my mother are married,' she said.

'With the greatest respect,' the ambassador said, staring at the matting as if it was the most fascinating thing he had ever seen, 'how would the Princess Mary know? She was not yet born.'

Mary swallowed, hard. This was unanswerable. He had made her look a fool. She was waiting, now, for her father to jump in and rescue her, telling the man not to be an ass, and telling the world that of course she was a proper princess, and totally legitimate, born within a marriage sealed by God.

But the pause continued.

Mary looked around, confused. Her father was staring at his hand as it lay clenched on the arm of his chair.

'I believed the queen and I to have been legally married,' he said at last. 'But it is true that God has failed to bless our union with children.'

Mary sat aghast, her mouth open like a fish's. She had heard him say this before, and each time it was painful. No children? But she was his daughter! How could he say that? She simply could not get used to the idea that a girl did not count as a child. How could he say that he had no children when she was sitting there right next to him?

Mary was glad, for a moment, that her mother was absent. Her mother would not be able to take this quietly, as Mary realised that she must. She turned her face aside so that the room would not be able to see her mouth quivering.

The pause lengthened. Mary could feel her face turning pink. She could scarcely get any air into her lungs, and found herself almost panting. All these people were looking at her and wondering if she really was legitimate!

The Frenchman cleared his throat.

'I understand,' he said, 'that the good lady the queen is Spanish. In that country, the custom is that women can inherit lands, thrones, crowns, with no impediment. Let us pay the Princess Mary the compliment of assuming, as a daughter of Spain, that this is true for her.'

The room, which had grown very quiet and still, came alive with nods and sighs of agreement. Mary would never have thought that the foreign ambassador would have saved her when her father could have done it. When she looked at his kind face, she found that her eyes were full of surprised, grateful tears. She hadn't noticed her father moving from his throne, but she now felt his hand grasping her shoulder.

'Good man!' he was saying, slapping Mary's shoulder in his offhand hearty way. 'Of course the Princess Mary is, for now, my heir. Just until my son is born.'

Mary relaxed, but only a little.

Why had he not spoken sooner? She felt that she was once again on solid ground, but it had not been her father who had put her there.

Chapter 4

22 June 1527, Hunsdon

Mary kicked her heels against the wooden frame of the bed, where she sat perched upon the feather mattress, moodily watching her mother brushing her hair. It was to be another fine day. She had begged and begged to be allowed to join her parents at Hunsdon Palace, rather than being sent off with her own servants to some other house as usual. It was much nicer living with her mother, and sharing her bed, than living in solitary splendour with just her own servants. It was much nicer having dinner with her father sometimes, too, and being three instead of one.

But now the king had just announced that his court was to move on again. Mary wasn't sure that she would be allowed to go with them to the next house.

'Why can't we just stay put?' she asked again, although she knew the answer.

'Because the food is all gone,' her mother explained. 'Our servants and you, yes you, hungry Mary, have eaten all the supplies of the villages round here. We have to forage! And, of course, your father says the game here is not good enough.'

Catherine made her last point in a mocking, ironic tone. Her husband's love of hunting had long annoyed her.

'Why won't he take us hunting with him?' Mary said petulantly, for the umpteenth time.

'Because we are too slow,' came the reply. 'You know that, Mary. You know that he has to ride fast.' Now Catherine sniggered. 'To keep down his weight, if nothing else. You know how he stretches his hands over his belly after Christmas, and says he can feel it has grown, like a woman's? Well, your father does his crazy sport and his hunting to keep his fine shape.'

Mary looked at her mother. The queen herself

had a magnificent shape, rather than an elegant one. But the summer sun pouring in through the window behind her caught her hair, which was still golden, and her gown was undeniably fine. She looks like an angel, Mary thought.

'Come on, Mary.' Catherine had done one of her unexpected switches from being the queen to being Mary's mother, as she so often did. Now she was chivvying Mary off the bed and into her slippers. 'I must call the ladies to dress you. We must get ready.'

'Can't we have dinner just you, me and Father?' Mary asked. 'I know, I know,' she added, 'a princess has to be seen to be believed.' She had seen her mother's mouth opening for a scold. Mary knew that she had asked too many questions already. 'But we always eat with the whole court watching,' she went on in a great rush, to get the words out before her mother could shut her up, 'and I never see just you and him by ourselves. Other girls have ...' Mary cast around for the word, not sure exactly what she meant. '... other girls have a *family*. You know, with parents, and brothers and sisters.'

Mary realised, too late, that she had mentioned the one thing certain to put her mother into a rage. She knew that her mother longed to give her brothers and sisters, but for some reason her mother's body just could not do it.

Would there be an explosion?

Mary saw her mother stiffen, as if she was clenching her self-control. But then Catherine slowly breathed out, and relaxed.

'You are seeing me now, *querida!*' she said lightly. 'That will have to be enough for you. And let's see a smile on that face or else the wind might change and you might get stuck that way. And what would the Duke of Orléans think then?' She was back at her dressing table, twisting her hair into a rope.

'It's not windy,' Mary said smartly. 'And I don't care about the duke.' This wasn't exactly true. She did care. But she knew it would please her mother if she was a little rude about her future French husband whom Catherine had not chosen. Mary was right. Catherine did smile, and made as if to tickle Mary with a long, pointed pin from her dressing table.

'Naughty,' she said indulgently. 'I'm going to use my pin to prick you under the chin. Let's see if that changes that sulky face!'

Mary shrieked, and retreated from the menacing pin. 'No, no!' she cried, laughing. 'Don't *pin* me, Mother! I'm not your mortal enemy! I don't want to fight to the death!'

She was soon rolling over and over in the unmade bed, getting all tangled up in the sheets, while her mother followed her with the pin. 'I'm going to *poke* you, Mary!' she joked. 'My pin's going to *tickle* you, Mary!'

'You blood-drinker!' choked Mary, coughing and laughing and by now buried under the coverlet.

All of a sudden, her mother was spinning away from her, the long pin drooping forgotten in her hand.

'What is it, Nan?'

Lady Anne Hussey was in the room. Probably they had missed her scratch at the door while they had been romping. It was Mary, much younger, who had mispronounced Lady Anne's name as 'Nan', and it had stuck.

'He's here, Your Majesty.'

Nan scurried to stand near the door, head bowed. She needed to say no more. Mary sensed her mother gathering herself, standing ready to present her usual poised curtsey. When others were present, the queen was always serene, always composed. And then her father was in the room.

'Catherine.'

He stood negligently while Mary's mother, on her knees, kissed his proffered hand.

'Are you not hunting, my love?'

'No,' he said shortly, spinning round to look out of the window. 'Going out in a bit.'

Mary realised that her father hadn't spotted her, hidden in the folds of the messy bed. It might be fun to go on hiding there a little longer.

But she could tell that he wasn't in a good mood. Even if his ignoring his favourite topic of conversation hadn't been enough, there was the tense set of his broad shoulders. Mary detected her mother's anxious movement towards him.

'What is it, my love? Tell me what it is.'

Her voice was smooth and silky. She'd turned on

that special voice she sometimes used, just for speaking to him.

But it didn't work. Even now he didn't answer.

'I've come to tell you something,' he said at last, still looking out of the window. Peeking out from under the sheet, Mary could just see the shape of her mother's bowed head. She watched and waited and said nothing. Mary was constantly astonished how her mother, usually so full of jokes and fun, could become a different, more serious person in her father's company. Although Mary was not sure that she preferred this other version.

'Tell me, my love.'

The words were just a soothing murmur.

Mary's father threw up an arm and rubbed at the back of his neck, as if it hurt him.

'I've decided,' Mary's father said abruptly, still looking out of the window, 'that our marriage is not legal.'

Mary herself almost gasped out loud. But in the room beyond the bed there was silence. Mary sensed rather than saw that Catherine's whole body had instantly stiffened up, and that she was standing and listening intently. The atmosphere in the sunny chamber had completely changed. It was as if the wind had come in and blown out all of Mary's petty little concerns about dinner.

'I suspected it,' her father continued, 'at the time those French ambassadors were at Greenwich. Do you remember, they pointed out that God has not blessed our union with sons, just as if God *is not happy with our union*? I think, perhaps, that is because it was illegal.'

'Henry!' It was a choked sound. 'How can you say such things? And in front of your child too!'

Mary raised herself to sit, hugging her knees and beginning to tremble with the awful passion that her mother seemed to be feeling as well. She covered her head, almost as if her father might strike her.

'Ah, Mary,' he said, noticing her. 'Well, it's right that she should know. Yes, our marriage was probably illegal. But I know that this was not your fault, *Catalina*, and you shall choose where you live once we part.'

Again, he had used the Spanish version of Catherine's name. Mary knew that he only did that when he was feeling tender, and she always listened out for it as the sign of a good day.

But now he pronounced it almost as if he felt sorry for her mother.

Mary opened her mouth to ask what on earth he meant. How could her parents possibly be parted? Surely, as married people, God himself had joined them together? But although her lungs had filled themselves with plenty of air, Mary couldn't seem to form the words to say anything coherent at all.

She could see that her mother's back was still straight, and stern, and not shaking by a single inch.

The long pause lengthened.

'Well?' Mary's father spun round in the end, raising his eyebrows, when his words met with no response. Mary shrank even further into the featherbed, expecting hard words or shouting. But she was surprised.

'I need legal counsel,' her mother said shortly. 'I know what my Spanish lawyers think, but I deserve advisors from among your own countrymen, those who are now my countrymen also. You cannot deny that that is fair.'

Mary's father seemed taken aback. He walked about the room a little, and seated himself in a chair. He was frowning and shaking his head from side to side.

'You have *already* taken legal counsel?' he asked eventually.

It was as if he couldn't believe it.

'Yes,' Catherine said crisply, folding her arms. 'I did so once it became clear that *she* was here to stay.'

With an awful sinking of the stomach, Mary realised at once that she knew who the 'she' was.

'And you are in danger, you know, from *her* religion,' Catherine said. 'You make a great mistake in thinking that our marriage is illegal under the law of the Holy Church. She's the one who talked you into that, isn't she? Her God is false and cheap. I can't think why she hates the good monks and sisters who pray for you every day. She will lead your soul into peril.'

As she completed her speech, Catherine's voice grew louder and faster. Mary couldn't see her mother's face, but she was sure that she was piercing her father with a gaze like a stiletto knife.

Mary thought that he visibly wilted. The wind seemed to have been taken out of his sails. He rested his chin on a fist and looked at the floor. There was more silence. Mary did not want to think any more about what her mother had just said. She could not think at all. There seemed to be clouds of smoke where her brain should be.

Something strong and dangerous was roiling up inside Mary. She knew that she shouldn't speak, that she hadn't been asked to speak, and that princesses were not called upon to give their opinions in council until they were married. But somehow she could not stay quiet any more.

She jumped out of the bed and ran across to her father, tugging at his elbow where it rested on the arm of the chair.

'We don't need any lawyers,' she said. 'Please no. Please. Please.' Without her even having noticed, she seemed to be crying. Tears were running down her cheeks. With a howl, Mary clutched her father's arm as if he were about to leave at once forever.

'Ah, *querida*!' Her mother was at her side, hugging her, giving her a kiss on the top of her head. Mary's father's hand was hanging awkwardly in the air, and her mother grabbed it and kissed it again, as she had done only a few minutes earlier. 'You're right, Mary, we don't need lawyers. We are your parents. We will always stay married, and together we will always look after you. Because we love you. Don't we, my lord king? Yes, we love you.'

Mary went on sobbing for a few minutes, before realising that she wasn't really crying any more, only pretending to. With a final hiccup, she lifted her face from her father's sleeve. He was ruffling her hair, and offering her his linen handkerchief. He was still looking shifty and embarrassed. Mary knew that he hated to see tears – he had often said so – and she began to feel ashamed. But mainly, she felt relief at her mother's words. 'Thank you, Mother,' she coughed. 'Thank you.'

Catherine smiled. Then she turned to face her husband, as if asking a question. The three of them were all still close together, on the chair and floor, but Mary could see that her father was straining away from them. He broke free and went to stand by the window again. Mary felt her panic coming back. He still hadn't said anything.

'I also came to tell you we're leaving Hunsdon tomorrow,' he said at last, a little distantly. 'And we will all ride together,' he said. He was more decisive now, as if he had made up his mind. 'I know you ladies will be a long time getting ready …' He sighed comically, and turned back towards them. 'But I will wait for you. We will go together.' Then he stepped forward, and again laid his hand on Mary's head. He puffed out his cheeks and bulged his blue eyes at her. It was a trick he had to cheer her up, and it never failed.

Mary smiled. It was enough. It was just about enough.

Nothing else had been said about the lady her mother had mentioned. But deep down Mary knew exactly who it was. It was the woman in the violet gown, of course. It was Anne Boleyn.

Chapter 5

February 1531, Greenwich

Mary is fifteen …

The next morning, the sun was shining, and all three of them rode together and raced each other along the green lanes. Her father had even let Mary win, while her mother laughed and scolded him as a daredevil.

Mary was hugely, agreeably relieved. Her father had once again called her mother 'Catalina', and 'bloody stubborn', and laughed at her, while Catherine and Mary together insisted that he had been riding too fast, and showing off.

But Mary's father wouldn't allow them to remain with his household for the whole summer. It was the hunting, he said. Catherine and Mary just couldn't keep up with the hours and speed at which he and his gentlemen rode. And accommodation was a problem too. Sometimes, his household and Mary's household and her mother's could just about fit into separate houses that were near to each other, but there often had to be days and nights when they were apart. Mary thought it was all silly. She didn't need her three hundred servants. She would much rather have had fewer, so she could stay more often under the same roof as her parents.

'No!' her mother said, when she suggested this. 'No! No! Your servants are your honour, Mary. You need honour, magnificence. It is all part of the battle.'

There she goes again, Mary thought sadly. *Fighting talk.* When her mother forgot to use her silky voice and hammered home her points like this, it made her father roll his eyes. It was much better to be peaceful and have fun, rather than to spend the days locked in deadly serious conversations with advisors and lawyers, as the queen now sometimes did.

'We don't need lawyers,' Mary would say to her mother when they were reunited at the end of those long days of meetings. 'You promised!'

'That's right, *querida*,' her mother would say. 'Your parents love you, don't forget.'

If she was feeling bored, or tired, Mary would deliberately call back the memory of her mother insisting that her parents loved her, that strange day of their quarrel at Hunsdon. Then she'd recollect as well how her father had fluffed up her hair and bulged his eyes and said that she could ride with him. It always made her smile. During the long weeks, and even months, when Mary was forced to live with just her own household, she needed memories like these.

***

Now it was winter, not summer, and the main court was back at Greenwich once again. This palace, at least, was big enough to accommodate them all, king, queen and princess, and their hundreds of servants too. And if Mary's mother wouldn't give her the right answer to the question of their living together more of the time in future, then maybe her father would.

Mary sat up on the bed where she had been lolling, thinking over the trials of her life, and decided to trot off and see him. He would be pleased, she thought, and might even call her his Mighty Princess and let her sit under his rug by his fire, the one made from the skin of a white bear. Sometimes, when she'd been smaller, he used to get beneath it and pretend to be the bear. She loved that rug.

The day was freezing, and Mary's own fire had died down. She'd been busy thinking, and when the pages had tried to bring more wood, she had called out that they should go away. It made her wonder, for a second, what it was like to live without three hundred servants. Was it rather lovely to make a fire for yourself? Was it rather satisfying to rely on just your own flesh and muscle? She thought that it might be.

Mary raised her cold fingers to her face and looked at them. God had given her these hands, but she never used them to do anything important. She spent so much of her life getting dressed, and sitting there while people looked at her. It seemed a waste, really.

Anyway, she could at least use her feet. To walk through the palace, she had to pass below the noses of the yeomen guards posted at each junction of the corridors and cloisters. She folded her arms across her chest and tried to scurry along unobtrusively.

But it was no good. They noticed her, inevitably, and drew themselves up and saluted.

What a palaver, Mary thought to herself. *I do wish they wouldn't.*

But then a nagging little voice in her head told her she was behaving badly, sneaking through the palace like a thief. She could almost hear her mother's voice telling her that she was on duty, was always on duty, and that she should have brought her ladies-in-waiting.

I don't care, Mary thought. Cold and defiant, she continued to slouch along.

Arriving at her father's rooms, she saw at once that he was out. She wilted a little with disappointment. The big chamber was deserted except for a couple of his gentlemen playing cards, and they stood silently and bowed at her arrival. These were gentlemen she knew well, but she eyed them suspiciously, as if they were keeping him from her.

'Princess Mary,' said one of them. 'Your Royal

Highness. What a surprise. What can we do for you?'

'Where is the king?' she said shortly, lowering her hands from her elbows and making an attempt to stand up straight.

'Hunting, hunting, always hunting!'

The gentleman spoke lightly, as if he were as bored as she was with her father's permanent absence. It almost made Mary smile back at him, although she could easily have snapped at him for disappointing her. Then she noticed a slight flinching of his face.

Mary turned to see what had caused it. A lady was coming out of the inner rooms. It must be one of the lower servants, Mary guessed, returning from a delivery of linen or beer or candles. But it wasn't. It was that nasty French-looking lady. Anne Boleyn.

As the lady came forward into the room, the two gentlemen bowed, and silently melted away out of the door. Mary would have said they almost oozed away, with no more sound than syllabub overflowing its bowl. But she could not help but notice they bowed lower to Anne Boleyn than they had done to Mary herself, at her own entry into the room.

The lady stood looking at Mary quizzically, her hands on her hips.

'Mary!' she said at last. 'What a pleasure. Come and sit with me and talk.'

Mary stood stock-still, unable to think what to do. There was nothing she wanted to do less than to sit and talk to Anne Boleyn. Everyone at court knew that the lady's father had recently been made an earl, and that she therefore now had to be addressed as 'Lady' Anne.

Anne Boleyn – Mary couldn't bear to call her Lady Anne, even within her own mind – now gestured at the stools placed near the fire.

Despite her reluctance, Mary couldn't think how to get out of the encounter. She shuffled towards the flames, and poked her raw pink fingers out from her sleeves to warm them.

Something was nagging away inside her mind. Why had the *Lady* Anne not said '*Princess* Mary'? That was the way she was always addressed. But probably it was just an oversight.

'That's better,' said the lady, in her curiously melodious voice, as they seated themselves in the flickering firelight. 'When I lived in France, we never had such barbarous weather as this.'

Mary wondered briefly what **Anne** Boleyn thought she was doing, making herself so at home in the king's outer chamber. They were breaking all sorts of rules by settling down and hogging the fire like this. Yet the lady appeared to be utterly at home here, stretching herself like a cat. Mary could not deny that the situation intrigued her. She knew that her father liked this woman, and that her mother hated her. But Mary's mother could be so ... *definite* in her likes and dislikes. What was the Lady Anne Boleyn really like? Perhaps this was the chance for Mary to form her own opinion.

'Tell me,' the lady purred, stroking the white fur trimmings on her black velvet sleeves as if to enjoy the delicious softness of them, 'what is your heart's desire?'

'My heart's desire ...'

No one had ever asked Mary such a thing before. She was quite taken aback. But wait a moment. Mary knew exactly what it was.

'My heart's desire,' she began, 'is that my father

66

should come and see me more often. Like he promised. But he's never where I think he's going to be.
Like today. I've come all the way over here for ...'

Mary broke off. She'd meant to say 'for nothing',
but that seemed rude, as she was now talking to
Anne Boleyn, which wasn't 'nothing'. Also, she felt,
perhaps too late, that she had conceded something
that she should not have done.

Information is power, her mother said, in a fight
to the death.

Anne Boleyn looked a little sad. Her long neck
drooped in a graceful arch.

'I know,' she said. 'It's hard to be parted from those
whom one loves.' Her eyes were big and black,
like those of a doe. She turned her head towards
the flames, as if to seek for those she loved among
the logs.

A strange and sudden pang of pity for the elegant,
regretful lady passed through Mary. It forced
her own eyes away from the flames and towards her
companion. Now, Mary saw, a tremulous smile was
playing on the lady's lips. She looked brave, Mary
thought. Beautiful and brave. Then she quickly

asked for God's pardon in her mind. Her mother would not, and therefore God would surely not, like her to think such things.

But her mother was not here.

'I can't see,' Mary said, emboldened, 'why my father has to go hunting so much of the time. My mother doesn't like it. I don't like it.'

'Why not?' came the careless answer. 'Your father loves the chase. It's one of his pleasures. He has so few pleasures, you know. So many cares.'

The words came out rather like the coo of a dove, rather than the speech of a normal human being. It crossed Mary's mind to wonder whether the cooing might not, after a while, become rather annoying.

'Well, he might fall off and hurt himself,' she said, feeling that this lady must be rather stupid. Everyone knew that her father was always breaking his bones doing his daredevil deeds.

'No!' The lady gave a tinkling laugh. 'I didn't mean that. How silly I am, not to express myself clearly. It's a gift. You have it, I don't. What I meant was, why doesn't your mother like your father to go hunting?'

Mary tensed. Why had she not said, 'Her Majesty, the queen', or even 'your mother, the queen'? Her mother had constantly cautioned her to be aware of every tiny infringement, and Mary had already let it slip once.

'Her Majesty,' Mary said, very quietly, knowing that she was doing her duty, but rather hating to make the correction in this intimate setting.

Although Mary had spoken softly, there was no doubt that Anne Boleyn had heard her. Of course, she must have ears like a bat. She was clearly one of those people who heard and saw everything.

'*Her Majesty*,' the lady repeated. 'Why doesn't *Her Majesty* like *His Majesty* to go hunting?'

By saying it in such an exaggerated way, Mary guessed that the Lady Anne was secretly laughing at her for standing upon ceremony. It wasn't such a pleasant feeling. She stood up, feeling ready to leave. She'd had no intention of getting drawn into this conversation with one of her mother's servants anyway. How on earth had it happened?

But there was no leaving. The Lady Anne's eyes

had a strange power. Now they were beseeching Mary, holding her in a hypnotic gaze.

'Have you ever wondered, Mary,' she asked slowly, 'whether you yourself are doing the right thing? You know, coming here, asking for your father, who is busy. You are being clingy, you know, and your parents don't like it.'

It took a few minutes for the words to sink into Mary's mind. This lady, this *servant*, had just criticised her! No one criticised her, ever. That was part of the deal. She clenched her fists. But then she relaxed them, almost at once. Of course, Lady Anne would notice if she reacted with hostility, and think her smaller for it. Her mother had trained her never to feel pain.

'Oh, and how do you know?' Mary said, with a silky smile like Catherine's. She imagined a snake, slithering its way through the grass. Nothing could upset a snake. She would be snake-like.

There was silence. Being snake-like didn't seem to be having the desired effect. Mary turned to see why the Lady Anne hadn't replied.

She was sitting there absolutely still, head bowed,

neck arched. But one arm was extended, just as if she'd been absolutely certain that Mary would eventually look at her. In her lifted hand was a letter.

Mary gasped. She recognised at once the wax seal, her mother's purple wax seal, which she always added before placing a letter in the hands of a messenger, pressing down upon the sticky, hot wax before it set with her big golden ring.

'How did you get that letter? It's from my mother!'

Mary felt herself as if teetering on the edge of some enormous void. This was wrong, all wrong.

But the lady still sat there mute, head bowed, eyes averted, holding out the letter.

The invitation to take the paper was overwhelmingly strong. Despite her confusion and anger, Mary was seized with an intense desire to know what it said. She tried to keep her hand by her side, but some irresistible power forced her to move it upwards, slowly, as if through thick gruel, to take the letter from the lady's hand.

She quickly flipped it open. Yes, she knew this writing. Yes, she knew that her mother always addressed her father with these fulsome compliments and statements and restatements of all his titles and honours; that was part of the stately game that she played so well. Her mother was always respectful. Or at least, she was always respectful until she lost her temper.

Mary's eyes moved quickly down to the meat of the letter.

You say, her mother had written, *that our palaces and our income are not large enough for three households, and that we should compress into two. You think that I will choose Mary, and go to live with her away from you. Well, my love, I will not. I will always choose you, you alone above all others.*

Mary read, stunned, scarcely able to believe the words.

In fact, she did *not* believe the words.

'This simply isn't true,' she said, with what she hoped was a scornful laugh. 'They promised that they would, well, always be happy, and live together, but with me too. They promised!'

But the lady was laughing too, faintly and falsely, a horrible sound. It sounded like a cat coughing.

'You are in error, *Your Royal Highness, my princess*,' she said, with exaggerated courtesy. 'Do you see the date on the letter? It is very recent. And do you see now the pain you are causing? Your father offered your mother an honourable way to leave court, to go away to live with you. But she did not do that. She did not choose you, she chose him. And this is very bad, very inconvenient, and it means that I too cannot live where and how I like, and this makes me sad. It is time to change, *Princess Mary*, and do as your father and betters ask.'

Mary knew that something was not right. She tried to grasp it, but her brain was working slowly, too slowly.

'Why would my father *not* want my mother and me to live with him?' Mary slowly spoke the words out loud, but her thoughts raced ahead. *He loves us both!* shouted a little voice inside her head. *He'd said we would live all three together.* Hadn't he? Hadn't he said that, at Hunsdon?

'He wants his freedom,' the Lady Anne said at once, with a kind of savage triumph. 'He thought your mother would choose *you*. And then he would be rid of both of you at once.'

This frightening lady seemed to have an answer for everything.

Mary stood shaking with rage and confusion. What could this mean? What had been going on behind her back? And finally, there came into her mind the question that she should have asked at once.

How had the lady got the letter? Had she stolen it? Surely Mary's father hadn't given it to her to read. Or had he?

She turned back, the question ready on her lips.

But it was too late. Without a sound, almost like magic, the lady had gone.

Chapter 6

February 1531, Greenwich

Mary was left behind, all alone on the white furry hearthrug. She was gasping like a trout brought out of the moat and on to the grass. She felt that all the breath had gone out of her, and left her limp, like a rag doll. At least, she thought foolishly, no one else had witnessed her humiliation. At least the room was empty.

At that very moment, though, Mary heard a gentle cough behind her. She whisked round. There, framed in the open doorway, was the outlined silhouette of a gentleman. Was it one of the oozing card players come back again? This was intolerable! She opened her mouth to speak sharply to him.

She could just imagine her mother's blazing wrath in the same situation. Mary thought that her mother often went over the top – but Mary hadn't felt goaded like this before.

But, before she could speak, the gentleman gave another polite cough, and came forth into the room. She saw now that it was Sir Nicholas Carew, a courtier who often paid his respects in her mother's apartments.

'My dear princess!'

His voice was full of concern, so much so that Mary found herself unable, or at least unwilling, to blaze with wrath. Her mind began, unpleasantly, to go over the conversation just past, and to calculate how much of it he might have overheard.

Sir Nicholas was coming across the floor now. He too had a little beard, but his face was swarthy, rougher than many of the gentleman courtiers' complexions. Mary knew that he spent a lot of time outside, with the horses. He was a great jouster.

'Princess,' he said, bowing again, and then, seeing that she was still choked up, he took her hand and led her gently back to the seat by the fire. He stood behind her, waiting, one hand on her shoulder. She felt calm flowing through him.

'Sir ... Nicholas.' She hiccuped, and quickly used her fingers to dash away some tears that had crept out on to her cheeks. She hadn't noticed them until now.

He whipped out a handkerchief, very clean and neatly folded. She grabbed it gratefully.

For once Mary didn't mind the lack of etiquette. She tried to half smile, but must have produced just a ghastly expression.

'I've had a bit of a shock,' she admitted.

'I know,' he said. 'I'm afraid I overheard. I know that was wrong, and that you are entitled to a private conversation. But your mother sent me to keep an eye on you. Once I saw *she* was talking to you, I was surprised, and I was worried for you. *She* is danger-ous, you know.'

Mary nodded her head, sadly. Yes, *she* was danger-ous. One part of her mind wondered how often her mother sent spies to watch upon her, but there was no time to worry about that now.

'I can hardly believe that my father *showed* her

my mother's letter. But how else would she have got it?'

He sighed. Although he seemed so easy to talk to, Mary could tell that he didn't want to answer.

'Princess,' he said slowly, 'something is going to happen to you very often as you get older. There will be bad news, and no one wants to be the bearer of it. Especially to a person, like you, who occupies a powerful position. Probably no one has told you something that I must tell you now.'

'Tell me what?' Mary felt almost angry with him, for keeping her in suspense, although she knew that he was trying to be kind. A little bit of her scoffed at 'powerful position'. She had no power at all, not even over where to go, what to eat, and when she could see her parents.

'Tell me!' she almost shouted, seeing him once again hesitate. He held up his palms, as if to beg for mercy.

'You know that your father, like all kings, has had … mistresses?'

Mary nodded. Her mother had explained this to her, years ago. When a queen was pregnant, as

Catherine often was, trying yet again to bear a brother or sister for Mary, then the king would go to the bedchambers of other women, to sleep there in their beds. It was not a big thing, Catherine had said, for he still truly loved Mary, and of course, Mary's mother. It was just for his health.

Mary realised that she understood this in abstract terms, but she didn't really understand what was involved. And certainly she didn't know who the mistresses were.

'Well, the Lady Anne is one of these mistresses,' he said, speaking so quietly that he was almost whispering, and Mary had to strain to hear. 'And she has gained great power over your father. He thinks himself in love with her.'

Mary realised that although nobody had told her, she had known this already.

'But,' she objected, 'are you sure? She's ... a *court* lady!'

'Yes,' Sir Nicholas said. 'He has been very tactless. Much better to leave his own wife's upper servants alone.'

He glanced around. Mary could tell he was afraid

that someone might hear. 'It is dangerous to speak of such things,' he said, 'but I respect and admire your mother – she is a woman of the good true Old Religion that I myself share.'

Mary sank slowly from her seat to her heels. She seemed to have lost all the strength of her body. She leaned down towards the stool where the lady had sat, and rested her head on it.

'What will happen to my mother?' she whispered, almost to herself. 'What will happen to her, if my father does not love her any more?'

She could feel the concern in his body, and the kind touch of his hand on her shoulder. 'She is a Spaniard,' he said. 'She will fight to the death. And I believe that she will beat this … woman, this … concubine.' He almost spat out the word.

Then it was as if he'd realised that he should say something more. 'And, of course,' he added quickly, 'whatever happens between them, they will both love you. Whatever happens between your mother and father, you are still the daughter of the king.'

Mary raised her forehead to look at him, only taking in the first part of what he had said, the part about fighting. Of course! Her mother had warned her that this would happen. That princesses always had to fight to the death. She'd never thought, though, that the battle would begin within her father's own privy chamber.

She looked levelly at Sir Nicholas, gathering all her strength.

'Thank you, Sir Nicholas,' she said calmly. She arched her neck, like a horse ready to trot proudly onwards. 'I am glad that you have told me the truth.'

He stood at once, and bowed again, placing his hand over his heart.

'You are your mother's daughter,' he said. 'That strumpet, that *woman*, with her cheap and dirty … *New Religion*, as they call it, will never get the better of you two. And don't believe that your mother rejected you,' he said. 'There has been some trickery with that letter, I'll warrant. You must ask her. Don't fear that your father wishes to set you aside, or does not love you. The whole court knows how proud he is of you.'

Mary bowed her head again. The effort of looking confident had cost her greatly, and all she wanted to do was to curl up under a sheepskin on her bed and think it all over.

Perhaps she could even get warm and go to sleep and hope to wake as if the afternoon had never happened.

As she stepped out over the threshold of her father's chamber, she sincerely wished that she had never come into it.

Chapter 7

May 1531, Windsor Castle

Sir Nicholas had advised Mary to question her mother about the letter, to find out what was true and what wasn't. But when it came to the point, she just couldn't find the words. What if her mother really had rejected her?

It was too difficult. Mary had to act so that her mother would ask *her* what was wrong. *I can manage to live all by myself,* Mary would say inside her head. *I am a daughter of Spain, who never feels pain. Even now, when my parents probably don't love me any more and want to be rid of me.*

She had somehow managed to set aside Sir Nicholas's warnings that the Lady Anne was capable of lies and treachery. She was worried that he had been too kind, and told her too much of what she wanted to hear. It was safest to assume the worst, to take the letter at face value. Her mother and father wanted to be without her.

Mary began to spend even more time by herself, skulking along the back corridors of the palace rather than face the constant discreet scrutiny of the guards. She would sneak to the gardens and walk there alone. And when her mother told her that she was outdoors too much, and ought to join the court ladies in embroidery, Mary said that she needed the exercise.

'You are growing lean,' Catherine said, worried. 'Your husband the duke will not like that. It is better to be bonny and buxom for the business of producing babies, you know.'

'And what would you know about that?' said Mary coldly.

She saw the hurt expression in her mother's eyes, and hardly cared at all.

I *care for nobody, no, not I, and nobody cares for me*, Mary sang inside her head as she marched off daily between the clipped walls of the Greenwich garden hedges. She had to tell Nan Hussey not to follow her. 'Leave me alone, Nan!' she barked. 'I'm not in any danger in the gardens. I want to … I want to just walk about by myself for once.'

There was just one friendly face in her memory, that of Nicholas Carew. Although palace life had never brought them together again, he smiled at her sometimes, across the Great Hall, or as she sat, sulking, in the ladies' box at the jousting tournament.

Mary assumed she would be sent off with her own household as usual when spring came. She even asked when she would leave.

'But Mary!' her mother said. 'Not long ago you were crazing and begging me that we might spend the summer together, both our households as one. So that's what I arranged. Are you not pleased?'

Mary couldn't deny the truth of this, so she made a sort of uncommitted mumble.

'I wanted to spend the summer with *my father*,' she added. It made her feel a tiny bit better to see her mother wince.

'Well, my darling,' her mother said, regaining her

cool composure. 'He is busy. And we will be together soon enough.'

In the spring, then, when it was time for Mary and Catherine and their servants to leave Greenwich, they rode together to Windsor Castle. Perched upon its hilltop, Mary loved this castle's dramatic skyline of towers and turrets. As they travelled, she saw that leaves were coming out on the trees, but later, and slower, and less lusciously than usual.

'It's been a hard year so far,' her mother said as they swayed up the hill in their litter.

Mary grunted.

'A *hard* year,' the queen said again.

Mary knew that she didn't just mean the cold weather. *This is what annoys my father*, she said to herself. *This is why he wants to be rid of us. She just can't let anything lie. She always wants to talk, talk about unpleasant things.*

But her mother hadn't finished. She gave a big sigh.

'Maybe,' she said, 'maybe here at Windsor we can make a fresh start, Mary. Can we be friends again?'

Mary's mother spoke simply, just like a normal

person, and Mary's throat suddenly tensed up painfully, as if she'd been asked to swallow a frog. How could she possibly answer such a difficult question? It was better to say nothing.

Mary turned aside and looked out of the litter. Now there were people each side, lining the road up into the town, and waving their handkerchiefs.

'Smile, Mary, I implore you! They are happy to see you.'

Mary noticed that as soon as they came within sight of the crowds, her mother's voice was transformed, becoming honey-warm. She was sitting up straight too, waving and kissing her hand, and responding to the people's good wishes on her side of the road.

You're not my friend, Mary thought to herself. *I don't really know who you are. You change from moment to moment.*

Mary couldn't bring herself to kiss her hand, and just sat there in stony silence. She scoffed in her mind at the idea that these people by the road might care about her. All *they care about*, Mary thought, *is seeing the rich dresses and the fine horses.*

She stole a glance at her mother's serene, smiling profile, still nodding and bowing to the Windsor townsfolk.

Mary remembered how a year ago she would have been delighted to be with the queen's household for the summer. But now she knew that she was only her mother's second choice.

A bitter voice started up in Mary's head as she began to remember and enumerate how many other things were wrong in the world. She remembered the humiliation of the evil snake-tongued lady knowing all the family's private business.

Another, more sober, voice in her brain told her that having the Lady Anne Boleyn to contend with was even harder for her mother than it was for her, and that she should have pity. But she didn't pay the sober voice any heed. It was difficult, all so difficult, when Mary knew that her mother didn't love her. And did her father love her or not? She had not seen him for so long.

The best Mary could do for the paupers who had gathered outside the entrance to the castle was to summon up a weak and watery smile. She took the coins her mother handed her and tossed them out with some energy.

That night, in the queen's rooms of the castle, overlooking the vast blue view, they were both busy with Mary's father's shirts. They were stitching the blackwork embroidery he liked round the neck and sleeves, something they had always done together. Mary's sewing was almost as neat as her mother's, and for a while the repetitive action soothed the nasty thoughts in her head.

She really hoped that her mother wouldn't start up again with the difficult questions.

But it was too late.

'Mary,' she began, without looking up. 'You know we make these shirts so carefully – do you also know that your father loves to receive and to wear them?'

Mary's head lurched up, like a deer catching the scent of the dogs.

'I know,' said Catherine, still looking down at her hands and working away methodically, 'that something has happened. That you are worried about something. Is it your father? Or is it me? You have not been the same for many months.'

It was true. But Mary shook her head, angrily. To her dismay, a couple of scalding-hot tears squeezed their way out from under her eyelids, and she could no longer see her needle.

Catherine threw down her linen.

'What is it, *querida*?' she asked again, gently. 'How have I deserved your displeasure?'

In a halting whisper, Mary started to speak.

'I saw your letter,' she said. 'I was in the king's rooms, and that lady was there, and she showed me a letter you wrote, saying you would rather live with him than me. That's why I suggested that I should leave. I know you don't really want me here. I know that you and my father and probably that lady too would all prefer it if I was out of the way.'

In an instant, Mary's mother threw down her embroidery, and flew across the room, and knelt by Mary's chair.

'My darling!' she said. 'How can you think that? I wrote that letter, but I didn't mean it. It was only for *politics*. I must stay near the king, because he is the source of all the power. If I am near him, and have influence, *then* I can keep you near me. Surely you see that? Surely,' she said, amazed, 'you see that I love you, more dearly than life itself, and that every action I make is guided by the thought of what's best for you?'

Mary's stomach lurched.

Oh, she had been so wrong.

Of course, she really had known this, underneath. Of course this was true. Why had she even, for one second, believed what the wicked lady had told her?

She hiccuped something about Sir Nicholas having said so.

'Oh, he is a good man,' Catherine said decidedly. 'If you want counsel, you can do no wrong with him. He is a man well able to see past the ... blinkers your father sometimes wears. Your father is so weak, so easily swayed by the opinions of clever people who get near to him. That's why I must stay close to him, always as close as possible, though it would be my heart's desire for you and me to go away, far away, and live quietly together. But to do so, in the end, would be our downfall.'

Mary coughed, and even came close to a little

giggle at her mother's over-the-top expression. 'Why would it be our *downfall*?' she asked. 'Why do we always have to stay and *fight to the death*? And when you write a letter, why doesn't it say the truth?'

'Because,' the queen said sadly, 'we can't always afford, in our position, to speak the truth. And because if we fall from your father's good grace, other people will trample upon us. It's the price of being a princess. Once you're a princess, you're always a princess. We can't go and live in a nunnery with the wise sisters the nuns – much as I would like that – because then other people would blacken our names, and seek to destroy us utterly. It is because I play the game well, the game of *politics*, that I believe that you and I will outlast all the other people who take advantage of your father. He will come back to us soon.'

Despite the trusting stare of her mother's fierce eyes, Mary made a mental reservation. Her father was not this weathervane figure that her mother described. He was the most powerful and strongest man that Mary had ever seen, breaking lance after lance in the jousting tournament yard.

Or he had been. It was an awfully long time since she had seen him.

It could be, she conceded, that the Lady Anne Boleyn had changed him.

'So,' she said, slowly, 'we will live at Windsor Castle and wait here, for my father to come?'

'Indeed we will,' her mother said, with decision. 'I think it will not be long, for I know that he doesn't have enough linen to see out the month. He has been travelling, and hunting, and seeing his friends, but remember this, Mary – he always, always, comes back for his new shirts when the time is right.'

Mary felt a little worm of hope stirring inside her. Perhaps he really would come back, like he had promised. Perhaps he would soon be calling her his pride and joy once again.

Nan Hussey was at the door.

'What is it, Nan?' Catherine was abrupt, annoyed at being disturbed. Mary looked down at the floor to hide her red, sore eyes, although she didn't know why she bothered when it was only Nan.

Nan could see that they had been speaking about something important.

'I'm sorry to interrupt,' she said, 'but here is a letter from the king. The messenger has just arrived. I thought that you would want to see it at once.'

'Oh!' Catherine got to her feet and bounded across the room to seize it. 'Just as I said, Mary. I'm sure he's writing to say that he's coming here soon. I told you so!'

Mary thought that in this candlelight, her golden hair glowing, her mother looked just as pretty as when she had been a teenage Spanish princess, marrying her handsome husband in St Paul's Church. It was a scene which her father had painted for her in words many, many times before.

'The most beautiful princess in Europe,' he used to say. 'My Catalina was, is, a golden girl.' She longed to hear him saying it again. Just like he used to.

When he said that, her mother would lower her heavy eyelids half across her eyes and give a lazy smile. If she was in a good mood, she would tell him not to be a snake-tongued flatterer from an Eastern bazaar.

Seeing her mother now, remembering this, Mary's spirits lifted. For the first time in months, it seemed, she felt the corners of her mouth creep upwards.

Catherine was reading now, having torn open the seal.

There was silence. Long silence.

'When does he arrive, Mother?'

'There has been ...' Her mother was speaking quietly, distantly, just as if Mary wasn't desperate to hear what the mysterious letter said. She spoke as if there was an unexpected minor inconvenience.

She trailed off into silence, reading quickly to the end of the letter.

'There has been a misunderstanding,' she began again, gathering herself and smiling up at Mary. 'We are to vacate this castle,' she said, 'for your father wants to come here with the Lady Anne, who has expressed a desire to see Windsor. And you and I are, for her convenience, to leave.'

'But we've only just got here!' Mary was dismayed. Leave Windsor? Not see her father? Not give him the shirts? She felt herself slipping back into the marshy quandary she'd been in before.

'Yes, we're to leave.'

Mary could tell that her mother was upset, but trying, for her sake, to put on an air of calm and decision. 'No matter. We are used to travelling.'

'And where are we to go?'

'Well …' Catherine seemed strangely reluctant to continue.

'I am to go to Cardinal Wolsey's house,' she continued, eventually. 'The cardinal has requested my company, it seems. And you, well, you are to go to the palace of Richmond. That's good. It's a fine palace, it's befitting to your status. Your father is paying you a compliment by sending you there.'

'But, if he wants to pay me a compliment, why doesn't he want to see me?' Mary asked. 'And we are not to go together? You said we had the whole summer together! You promised!' Mary had forgotten all her previous suggestions that she should go away with her own servants.

Mary could hardly believe her father's reasoning. Why were the Lady Anne's wishes so important? Surely they weren't more important than the wishes of the queen and the princess of England?

Why was her father acting as if they were? As if he truly preferred the Lady Anne?

'I'm sorry, darling.' Catherine finally turned to Mary, and Mary could see that her eyes were glinting, too, with tears that she was attempting to hold in. Mary could see how hard her mother was trying to be brave.

Mary knew, in that instant, that her mother would never forswear her, or reject her.

'We'll manage,' she said softly, reaching out a hand as if her mother were the child.

'The time of a great test is coming, my love,' said Catherine, with a sigh. 'You will be stretched, oh, ever such a long way. You'll be stretched until you think you might break in two. But I will send my people to protect you as best I can, and you must always trust me. The wicked lady seeks to part us,' Catherine continued. 'But remember, Mary, in my mind I am *always* with you. Your father does still love you, I know he does. And remember that I love you fiercely.'

'Of course you do, you blood-drinker,' Mary said. And for a moment they both managed a little smile.

PART TWO

IN
EXILE

Chapter 8

April 1533, Beaulieu

Mary is seventeen ...

How Mary regretted those three long months between February and May when she hadn't been speaking to her mother!

She was walking about in the garden, walking fast so that her household officers would think she was exercising and not interrupt her.

Mary, as always, was thinking about her mother. She had not seen her for two years now, two long years of living by herself. Or at least, living by herself, but for a couple of hundred servants. And Nan. Sometimes at night Mary would wake up suddenly to find tears wet on her face. She knew then that she had been dreaming, yet again, of riding down the hill, away from Windsor Castle with Nan, trying not to cry.

Since then she and Nan had been at Richmond, and at other palaces, and now at Beaulieu in Essex. Each one of them was very grand, but they seemed to Mary to be magnificent prisons. It was all very well having fine chambers to live in, and gardens in which to walk, but she hadn't managed to learn her mother's trick of running a household well. However hard she tried, the fires were always unlit, and the guardsmen's uniforms a little rumpled.

'Your mother would call in the senior officers each morning,' Nan told her, 'and tell them their duties for the day.'

'What, every morning? When did she read her books?'

Nan sighed.

'She did not spend as much time reading as you do, my princess. In fact, no one does.' As Nan had known Mary's mother for longer than Mary had, she seemed almost like a second mother. Only less demanding. It had been Nan whom Mary had gone to when she started to bleed; it had been Nan who sometimes came in and comforted her when sad dreams woke her up at night.

Mary knew that she should try harder to behave more like a princess, but it seemed less and less worth the effort. Who would know how many of her attendants served her at meals? But then, when Cardinal Wolsey's servant arrived unexpectedly with a letter from her mother, just at the hour of dinner, she knew that he had observed her lazy lack of state. She knew that he would report back to the main court, and thus to Mary's father, that the princess had been eating her dinner with Nan alone, and had let the gentlemen of her household have the evening off.

Mary grew warm as she walked, and touched the cold, wet leaves of the rosemary bushes to cool down. She ought to walk more, ride more, read less. Her mother, she thought, would stiffen her spine, put a little Spanish fire into her everyday life.

But when would she see her mother again? Here at Beaulieu, the letters had been few and far between, and sometimes they did not quite make sense. Mary suspected that some of them had failed to arrive.

She had the feeling that the wicked Lady Anne, so powerful now at court, had means of causing messages to miscarry, of making servants misunderstand their directions. Mary ground her teeth together. She was so tired of thinking of the wicked lady. Her image in Mary's mind was the flip side of her mother's: Catherine was day, Anne was night. One always followed the other.

But then, Mary consoled herself, they simply had to sit this out. It would be all right in the end. Her father needed mistresses for his health, her mother had said. Surely he would put the Lady Anne aside in the end, just as he had done with mistresses before. It was a refreshing thought, like the sharp scent of the needles of rosemary Mary had been pinching between her fingers.

She heard a tentative tread on the gravel behind her, and turned around with a sigh. What was it now? It was Nan's husband, Sir John, or to give him his full name, Sir John Hussey. Probably he wanted to know whether he might appoint a new kitchen boy, or let go one of the more wasteful maids. Mary quickened her pace, hoping that he would take the hint and leave her alone. Such decisions could wait until dinner time.

'Princess!' he was calling in his weedy voice. Nan was familiar, comforting, solid as the hills, but her husband was a bit ... ineffectual. Mary wished that there was more substance to him, and that he could make up his mind more often by himself. Her own father, she guessed, would be infuriated by Sir John's drippy ways. He was always so decisive – well, at least about small things.

Mary stopped, and sighed loudly. She would let him know that he had annoyed her. But as soon as she saw his expression, she knew it was something more serious than the usual household trivia. He was holding a letter, a big one, and he was waving it towards her so that she could see the seal. It was an enormous red seal. Just like the wax seals her father's secretaries used.

Mary gasped, and almost ran towards him. He was smiling at her eagerness, for sometimes, despite her moods, she reverted to being a little girl.

Mary held the letter in her hands for a minute, and he started to back off.

'No, Sir John,' she said, feeling generous for once. 'Stay here and read it with me. It might contain a direction for us to move once more.' If that was the case, then it would be Sir John who would give the orders for the household to pack and to travel.

Calm down, Mary said silently to herself as she broke the seal. *It might equally well contain bad news.* Ever since her mother had so confidently opened that letter at Windsor which had broken her heart, Mary had had a horror of sealed paper packets like this. In fact, come to think of it, she had a bad feeling. Would it be possible not to open the letter at all?

'Sir John, why don't you read it for me?'

Now he sighed. He was always so full of fuss that he didn't like being asked to do something that he thought even one inch out of the ordinary.

'If you insist, madam,' he said reluctantly. 'It might be private.'

Mary thrust the letter back towards him, holding it loosely so that it was in danger of falling to the gravel. Actions speak louder than words. Her father had said that once, when he had bounced and dandled her on his knee in the Great Chamber, even when she'd been a bit too big and had found it undignified. 'I'm doing this, Mary,' he'd said, 'because I love you, and because I want everyone to see that I love you.' The memory made her a little sad. She could scarcely believe he loved her still. No, that wicked lady was his new love, and had taken up all the room in his heart.

Her gesture with the letter worked.

Sir John was opening the seal, sighing a little as he did so, and shaking his head. He was still shaking away as he puzzled out the words. Mary smiled. Her father, unlike her mother, hated writing, and never took the trouble to make his words clear.

In the end, she gave up waiting. Mary was more used to her father's hand; she took the letter back. But Sir John was still looking inquisitive. All right, she would tell him what it said.

'Sends his best wishes,' Mary summarised. 'Hopes I am in good health and not bothered by the airs of Essex. He never liked this county,' she explained to Sir John, 'which is quite ridiculous, as its air is no different to Suffolk, or even to Greenwich if it comes to that.'

She saw she had confused him. 'All right, all right!' she said, laughing. Honestly, he was such a worrier. 'Back to the letter.'

'He sends the good news that the French ambassador has been to London again ... oh, and that his horse Zorro has been ill but now is well. Really, I wish he would get to the point.'

Sir John interjected.

'But madam, surely it is good for us if His Majesty cares to update us with all the court news?'

She knew what he meant. The courtiers were always reading the runes, finding meaning in the smallest detail. But surely her father would have some special message, just for her? Surely it would not all be about the illness of his horse?

'And then he says ... he says ...' Mary broke off once more. This was quite a change of key, in the sentence at the end. She looked at the ground, and then the bushes, then back at the letter. Yes, it still said the same thing.

'He says,' she continued, gathering herself, 'that he has married. He has married again. I mean, he says he has married the Lady Anne Boleyn.

But that cannot be true, for he is married to my mother.'

Mary's voice failed her. It could not go on reading. There was a dismaying gap in her mind where her thoughts should be. Sir John's doglike eyes were large and moist, and looking at her with intense concern. Mary couldn't bear it. She avoided them by looking back at the letter.

'He says that,' she went on, in a tiny croak, 'that in the light of the situation, it would be improper for me to write or to receive letters from, from, the dowager ... Who does he mean? Does he mean my mother? And that he looks forward to introducing me to my new mother soon.'

Sir John had never surprised anyone in his life, but now he surprised Mary.

He spoke softly, politely, slowly shaking his head, so gently that Mary could scarcely believe her ears when she took in the actual words.

'*That woman*,' he said, 'is a bitch. A bitch of the highest order. I must tell you, Your Royal Highness, that this is unlawful. I am sure it is unlawful.'

'I ... I suppose so.'

Mary wasn't sure what to think. Didn't her father *make* the law? She felt quite at a loss, scarcely able to take in the horrible thought that *the wicked lady* was so firmly ensconced in her mother's old place, by her father's side, in his chambers, in his bed. How on earth had her father allowed that to happen? There was something wrong with him. He had been deceived. The Lady Anne had deceived him.

'It is wrong, wrong.'

Mary had never seen the hangdog Sir John Hussey look more put out. The letter, its contents, seemed so unbelievable. It was Sir John's expression, as much as anything, that convinced her that this was really happening.

'This cannot be allowed,' he said, speaking almost firmly. 'You are forbidden to communicate with your mother, are you? Well, I am not. And neither is my wife. We will find out her wishes for you, princess, never fear.'

He turned to lead her back towards the house, but Mary seemed to have difficulty in putting one foot in front of another. He took her arm, as if she were not well.

'This is bad news,' he muttered again. 'But it clarifies things, princess. This is open war,' he continued, 'and your father will find that your mother has many strong allies. And he will find out that this so-called new *church* of his, the one which has given him permission to marry when our true Church of Rome did not, will not withstand the smallest assault.'

Mary noticed that he was using the language of battle.

'Oh yes,' she said. 'My mother will fight to the death. I believe that. We must find out from her how best to behave.'

She stopped, realising that there was no hesitation in her mind that she was going to disobey her father's orders. She was going to disobey the orders of her king. But it was all right. He wasn't himself just now. She imagined him popping, bulging his eyes out to make her laugh. Yes, one day he would be back to normal, and making her laugh again.

'That's right,' Sir John said. 'That's right. Your mother will fight to the death.'

It sounded almost ludicrous, said in his mournful

tones, but Mary couldn't laugh. It was too serious. How was she going to find out what her mother wanted her to do? When would she see her mother again?

Sir John was suddenly kneeling before her, his hand on his heart.

'My wife and I,' he said unexpectedly, 'really … we worship your mother. She is a wonderful lady. We will dedicate ourselves to her daughter until her, and your, rights are truly recognised, as they should be.'

Mary reached out and touched his hand to raise him up. He was a soft sort of ally, but he was shaking with emotion. He really meant it.

'Thank you, Sir John. I shall need your support.'

She was embarrassed, but she really meant it too. She'd need all the support she could get.

Chapter 9

December 1533, Beaulieu

They were having their dinner, Sir John, Lady Nan, and Mary. She had taken to eating with them, breaking bread even though she knew she should not with people who were her inferiors in rank. Of course, Mary should really only have sat at table with her mother or father. Or with the brothers and sisters she wished she had. But frankly, she could no longer bear to eat alone.

The loud knocking at the door made them all pause, Sir John in the very act of tearing open a roll, Nan with her goblet halfway to her lips. They all knew that sound. It meant trouble. It meant a messenger, from Mary's old home. From the court, from the palace, where Anne Boleyn was now living Queen Catherine's old life.

Mary and the Husseys had been expecting someone to come from court, ever since they'd heard that a baby had been born to ... to her father's new wife. Mary couldn't bear to call her Queen Anne, even in her own head. And she couldn't bear to think of that baby girl, her own half-sister, her replacement. The visitor must be someone with the clout to frighten Mary's servants into allowing access straightaway, rather than going through the rigmarole of waiting politely in the outer room until the princess should be pleased to admit the supplicant.

They quickly looked at each other, and Mary rose, wiping her lips with her napkin. She spread her hands on the tabletop and nodded to Sir John.

'Enter!' he cried out, in what Mary knew was the boldest voice he could manage.

It was the Duke of Norfolk, long, skeletal and ghostly with his pale face. He came shuffling into the room, bowing in a perfunctory fashion to Mary, scarcely acknowledging Sir John and Nan.

'My lady,' he croaked. His voice, never very pleasing, sounded even more rasping than Mary remembered, rather as if a skeleton was speaking. It occurred to Mary what a long time it was since she had seen him at Greenwich, at court in the old days, and how much older he had become.

'I am "Your Royal Highness",' Mary said at once to the Duke of Norfolk coldly, 'not "your lady".' She decided to correct him immediately, thinking that attack was the best form of defence.

Sir John, in his conscientious way, had briefed her about this. Her mother had written to her, secretly, about this very point. Now that she had a rival for her position as her father's beloved daughter – this new half-sister, Elizabeth – she must stand on her dignity at all times, and insist on all her honours.

The duke gave a half smile.

'Well, you open up the matter at once,' he said, clutching his gown a little closer around his spare person.

'Cold, Your Grace?' she said courteously. 'Do come and sit here, near the fire.'

Mary sensed Sir John smiling into his beard, approving.

It cheered her, as if she had scored a little point in a game. Old men were invited to sit by the fire; the duke was an old man. She had just been ever so slightly disrespectful.

But the duke wasn't to be diverted, and remained planted in the middle of the room, leaning a little on his white staff.

His rheumy eyes tracked around the chamber, noticing, Mary was sure, crumbs on the floor, and embroidery wool in a mess on the sideboard where it had no place to be.

Mary continued looking at the duke narrowly, inviting him, by her silence, to get on with what he had to say.

The duke made the concession of bowing his head, and began.

'I am instructed,' he said, 'by your royal father, to instruct you in your turn that you are to begin a new mode of life.' He paused to let that sink in. Mary quickly glanced at Nan. Yes, she was looking surprised too.

'You are to travel now to Hatfield House,' he continued, 'there to enter service. You will become a lady-in-waiting to the princess, your half-sister that is, the young Princess Elizabeth. You will no longer be known as princess, obviously, for that is no longer your status now that your mother is no longer queen. You will be known as … the Lady Mary.'

Mary was glad to feel the rough wood of the table beneath her fingers. It reminded her to brace her muscles, not to sway. She was surprised, but not shocked. *So, it's happened*, she told herself sternly. *At least it has happened. I don't have to dread the thought of it happening any more.*

This was *exactly* what her mother had warned her about. Tight against her skin, under Mary's stays, was a secret letter, delivered in the middle of the night by their good friend Sir Nicholas Carew, preparing her for exactly this eventuality. The day had come!

For a moment Mary's brain whirred, stupefied. What was she to do? *Remember*, she told herself fiercely, *you can remember the instructions.*

Her mouth opened, almost of its own accord, and she began to speak, trying to keep the shake out of her voice.

'Your Grace,' she said, smooth as silk. 'I will go to pack for the journey at once.'

She turned her back on him, no curtsey, no, that would be wrong from a princess to a duke, nodded at Nan and Sir John, and immediately left the room.

Nan was hard on Mary's heels. She stopped in the room beyond, just to catch her breath.

'Well done!' said Nan. 'You did it perfectly! You were polite but firm, and you agreed at once to what he asked.'

Mary remembered how she had seen one jouster compliment another after a good run on the tournament. This was a tournament, that was all. She knew the rules; she had her tactics prepared. She smiled at Nan, and together they went on.

They went as quickly as possible to Mary's bedchamber, and spent a frantic few minutes searching for ink.

'Good Lord, I must keep my things in better order,' Mary said, annoyed with herself.

'It's here, it's here, stay calm.' Nan was bringing the jar over to the table where Mary had a piece of paper ready. Mary's hands were wobbling a little, so she rubbed them together, to remind them to behave.

She began to write, then looked back at what she'd done. No good. Spidery. She shoved the sheet aside and began again, with bolder, blacker strokes. Her mother had told her exactly what words to use. Twenty minutes later she was finished.

And twenty minutes later, there was a knock at the door. Sir John.

'I cannot hold him any longer,' Sir John confessed. 'He demands your presence. He says that half an hour is enough to pack necessaries, and that you must come down at once.'

Mary arched an eyebrow and stretched in her chair. She had been writing hard, and it felt good to release her grip, and good to have finished.

'That's all right, Sir John,' she said, 'we're ready.'

All three of them exchanged a glance, and a nod, and then they were on their way back down. In the chamber, the duke was pacing, tapping menacingly with his stick.

Mary seated herself back at the table on the dais, back straight, hands folded in her lap. She nodded at Nan.

'Lady Anne Hussey has a statement to read out.'

Nan stood, curtseyed, unfolded the paper and began. There was a lot of legal verbiage, copied verbatim from Mary's mother's draft. Then there was the key sentence.

The princess accedes to what she is commanded to do by her father, His Majesty the King. But in doing so she does not concede any challenge to her status. Legally, she was, is and always shall be the princess of England. What she may be forced to do under duress does not compromise this.

The duke had stopped his pacing to listen, but now he began to prowl once again. Mary could tell that he hadn't been expecting this.

'I …' he began. He stopped.

'I … believe you have made your position clear,' he muttered at last. 'And now we are to leave.'

Lady Anne spoke.

'*The princess*,' she said deliberately, 'requires more time for the readying of her possessions.'

The duke snapped.

'No more time!' he barked. 'You have had half an hour. You did not spend it wisely. I am commanded to send this … this young lady to Hatfield as soon as may be. *With all speed.* It was His Majesty's specific command.'

'With respect, Your Grace.'

Now Sir John was speaking. His hangdog manner was mollifying and obliging. 'It is no little thing to transport a household of scores of servants with only half an hour's notice.'

'Ah, but the Lady Mary will not be requiring her household.'

Mary, Lady Anne and Sir John looked at each other in consternation. This was an unexpected new turn. Did he want Mary to go to Hatfield … by herself?

The duke noticed their faces.

'Yes,' he said firmly. 'As the Lady Mary will now be her sister the princess's servant, she will not require servants of her own. It would be unfitting. And now, my lady, my men are here to escort you to your horse.'

With that, the door swung open.

As the duke beckoned, a great many menservants in livery came storming into the room. Their faces were blank. They were well dressed, in suits of dark wool – sober, respectable men. But they were many in number, and strangely silent.

Mary looked at them, and knew she was beaten. Silently, she rose, and stepped forward.

Nan started to follow her.

'But the princess's clothes!'

'No!' barked the duke, holding up a hand. 'You had your chance. You didn't get the clothes when you had the chance. And you're not coming. Just the Lady Mary.'

Nan stood silent. Mary could imagine her opening and closing her mouth like a fish, a habit she sometimes had.

'I will send for you hereafter,' Mary called out, as confidently as she could, even though she was now half out of the door. 'Don't worry! I'm sure I will be safe!' She said this to shame the duke and his men, who were frightening her. The men were stepping very close to her, not actually touching her but surging her along with their own motion. She squeezed in her arms, to avoid brushing their sleeves.

'We will await your commands,' cried Sir John. 'We will be following you soon, my princess!'

And with that the door swung shut behind Mary.

Then the afternoon became a blur of horses and spurs and saddles and an unfamiliar great cloak wrapped over her dress. Within minutes, Beaulieu was behind her. And except for these scores of strangers, Mary was all alone.

Chapter 10

December 1533, Hatfield

Some hours later, they were riding up yet another muddy lane, and then through a park scattered with the leafless skeletons of fine big trees. Mary could see a church, and a cluster of houses. Despite her fear and loneliness, she looked around with some interest. What was this new place? She was used to travelling from palace to palace, but usually with the same familiar wagons, and people, and possessions. This was a whole new world.

She was cold, even inside the rough and heavy cloak of black and brown checks. It was more like a shepherd's blanket than something a princess should wear. And yet she was glad to have it. The ride had been misty, and now a wintry dusk was falling. She was riding on the pillion seat behind the broad back of a man she didn't even know, leaning back as far as she possibly could to minimise touching him.

As they passed a dark, low huddle of houses, Mary could see people looking out anxiously from lighted doorways. She caught a glimpse into a stable, and saw a man among his cattle. She saw a little girl being snatched indoors by a woman swathed in shawls, her face averted.

Mary knew that a body of horsemen, riding through the dusk, was something that these people feared. And rightly so. It certainly meant trouble, of one kind or another.

She herself was terribly anxious about what would happen next. All through the journey, her mind had kept travelling to the palace at Greenwich, wondering what was happening there. Surely her father couldn't know what was being done in his name? Surely he couldn't have meant for her to be treated like this? She ached to see him. Or her mother. She had been alone before, but this was as if she wasn't part of the family at all.

Ahead, over the roofs of the houses, she could see what looked like stars floating in the darkness. With a start, she realised that they were the lighted windows of a gallery, presumably high up in a building that was almost invisible against the sky. This must be a huge house.

Mary, a courtier, read the message at once. This new princess, the Princess Elizabeth, had been given a better house than Beaulieu. And now Mary didn't even have Beaulieu, either.

What would Sir John and Nan Hussey be doing there now, aghast and sad? Mary guessed that they would be writing at once to Mary's mother, or maybe the Spanish ambassador, for advice. Maybe they'd even contact the ambassador of the Holy Roman Emperor, her mother's nephew across the sea. She was comforted by the thought that a web of loyal friends would look out for her mother and her. It was a web that her father's remarriage had woven even tighter. The web was united by loyalty to Catherine, yes, but also to the old God whom Catherine had taught Mary to worship.

One of Mary's worries about coming to Hatfield was, would there be a priest for her? Would they want her to attend Mass according to the coarse, crude New Religion that Lady Anne had made popular at court? If she went to one of the new Masses, it would be a danger to her soul. She must never, ever do that.

I *promise, Mother,* Mary said in her head. I *won't do that.*

Suddenly, out of nowhere, she felt a little warmer, and a little easier in her mind. It was as if someone had laid a calming hand on the throbbing thoughts in her brain.

And now they were arriving, and men were lifting her down off the horse, and her cold, stiff feet were giving way beneath her as she tried and failed to regain her footing.

The house had a wide flight of steps between its courtyard and its door, and Mary stumbled as she climbed. It was utterly dark now in the cobbled courtyard, except for a burning torch held high by a servant. A slice of light that came shooting out from the open doorway of the house confused Mary's eyes.

Beyond the door, she discovered, there was a passage, then a panelled Great Hall. A great heap of logs was burning brightly in its vast fireplace, along with throngs and throngs of lit candles. Mary had forgotten what a sight it was to see a room so illuminated. The hall was festooned with garlands of leaves and laurels. Mary could see that everything was set for a joyful twelve days of Christmas festivities. It was a time of year that her father loved, and the sight of the candles made her think of his rooms at Greenwich, lit up like this for a party.

On the table stood the remains of a huge ham, peeking pink and studded with cloves. Mary's stomach rumbled a little. It had been a long time since the midday meal that the duke's arrival had denied her the chance to eat.

But who was in charge? Surely there would now be gentlewomen to direct her. She would be offered hot water for washing, maybe some warm wine or posset. Posset! Yes, that would be lovely. She almost turned to Nan to suggest it, before remembering that for once she had no gentlewoman with her. She was alone.

Mary stood, blinking, unsure what to do.

Then, with tremendous dignity, two figures were rising and advancing, one down each side of the long central table. A man and a woman. For a second Mary thought it was the Husseys, come miraculously to her aid. But these people were more stylish, better dressed, indeed almost as chic as the French ambassadors. For a stunned second, Mary was drawn into admiration of the slick, sleek cut of the lady's black gown.

'Lady Shelton,' said the man, gesturing. 'My wife.'

But Lady Shelton simply stood there, not offering, not welcoming, not leading. It was almost as if she were waiting for something.

Mary still stood uncertainly, looking round the room for a clue. It was odd not to be able to find someone to guide her in what to do next.

The man raised his eyebrows.

'No curtsey?' he said. 'My lady wife is the mistress of the household of the Princess Elizabeth, you know. That means that she is *your* mistress.'

Mary understood at last. *She* was expected to consider herself as inferior to these people! *She* was expected to curtsey!

And she knew the name. She chased it through her memory. Lady Shelton ... this was the demonic Anne Boleyn's aunt. The man must be Sir John Shelton, her husband. Anne Boleyn had put her aunt in charge of her daughter's nursery.

Lady Shelton arched her long neck, and waited.

A slight trembling began in Mary's legs, as if the sheer force of their expectation was going to make her curtsey, against her wishes. This was ridiculous! She must resist!

There was a long silence.

'I wish to go to my chamber,' Mary said. 'And I wish to summon my waiting woman, Lady Anne Hussey, at once. I should not have been brought here against my will without her.'

'Oh dear. You certainly will not.' Sir John Shelton sounded almost sorrowful that she had behaved so badly. 'You must understand, my Lady Mary, that *you* are now the waiting woman. And you will be wanting to go to pay your respects to the Princess Elizabeth, surely, before you go to your chamber?'

Mary stood, mute. This was horrible. What should she do?

She felt a single hot, humiliating tear slide down her cheek.

Then she heard something inside her head, again something that warmed and comforted her. It was the honeyed voice of her mother. *Stand up straight, Mary!* it whispered. *You are the daughter of Spain.*

It worked like a miracle. She turned away from the Sheltons at once, rudely showing them her back. She knew what a shockingly disdainful action this was, and it gave her almost a thrill.

Mary swept out through the arch, back into the passage. Here there were lesser servants, serving men and serving women. They would be less flinty and immutable. They would help her.

She would just have to show them that she needed help.

'Tell me where my chamber is,' she said, not troubling to keep the tears out of her voice. *Actions speak louder than words*, she told herself. She needed sympathy now. She swayed, almost as if she was about to faint.

'Of course.' A woman in the rough woollen gown of a serving maid stepped close and took her arm.

'The Lady Mary is not well!' she said loudly. 'She is faint. She must lie down at once!' There was a buzz and a bustle of consternation.

Underneath its cover, the lady whispered something. 'My princess. Do not fear. You have some friends here.'

Mary almost gasped with the surprise of it. Had she heard correctly?

'Quick!' the woman said, even more loudly. 'She almost fainted!'

At that Mary felt the grasp of hands at her elbows, and, leaning on the strange maid's arm, she was swept out of the entranceway, and through rich rooms to a staircase.

Upon it were wooden figures, curiously carved, hard to see in the gloom. She wondered which way the baby Princess Elizabeth's chambers were, and prayed that she was not being taken towards them. But no, the swarming hands were guiding her up, and up again, past the principal floor where surely the best rooms lay.

Up again, they were still climbing, and then they were in that lighted Long Gallery Mary must have seen from below. She was taken to its far end, and through a pokey little door in the corner. Inside was a chamber, perfectly fine for a servant, perhaps, but not at all sumptuous. It didn't even have tapestries on the walls, just a cloth painted with a forest instead.

It contained a bed, just a little low wooden bed, close to the floor. But never had a sight been more welcome. Mary sank down upon it, still in her smelly cloak. She rested there, facing the wall, ignoring all the bustling servants who had accompanied her.

I'll just lie here looking ill, she said to herself, *until they leave me alone.*

She wondered for a second what God would think of her duplicitous behaviour. *I'm only half pretending*, Mary quickly reassured Him in her mind. She really did feel faint and sick as well as lonely and confused.

The friendly serving woman was outside the door, and Mary could hear her fending off other enquiries and servants.

'I think we should let her rest,' she was saying. 'Sir John and Lady Shelton will certainly want to see her again in the morning. Let her gather her strength until then.' The voices gradually died away.

Unwillingly, Mary opened her eyes, rolled into a sitting position, and began to look round her room. It seemed as if she was staying here, at least for the night.

Slowly, she swung her legs to the floor. Yes, this was a bed, and she was grateful for it, but she was used to a canopy and curtains, not a low box bed like this. The bolster was rough, hairy linen, and inside it she could feel the prickle of straw, not feathers.

She lifted the single candle that had been left burning by the bed, and began to explore. There was a chest to contain the clothes that Mary had not brought. There was no sign of any clothing waiting for her here, and it flashed across Mary's mind that she had only one set of linen. Would she have to wear it again tomorrow? That was rather horrible. She knew that the common people did such things, but she had never in her life done so before.

Time passed. The slight sounds of people coming and going in the gallery penetrated Mary's chamber, and so did the cold from the night outside. She took one of the blankets off the bed, and wrapped it round her over the black-and-brown cloak. She found she was shivering, and stood up to try pacing about a bit to get warm. It struck her that she was something like a prisoner. But the door wasn't locked, of course.

Or was it?

It turned out that Mary *could* lift the latch, and she peered out into the gallery. A gentleman usher was waiting there, seated on a wooden stool and tossing a small item – was it a toothpick? – from one hand to another, as if bored.

Perhaps an hour or so had passed already. She wasn't quite sure. Certainly he looked like he had been there a long time, and expected to remain.

Mary's heart sank. There was no sign of the friendly serving woman in grey, who had whispered a secret welcome. But at least it was neither of those terrifying Sheltons, sharp and cold as steel. Mary shuddered at the thought of them. She had behaved rudely and offended them, and she was in their house. How would they respond when she saw them next, as surely tomorrow she must?

Although Mary had opened the door as quietly

as possible, the man outside it had noticed that she was looking out. He quickly stood, and bowed.

'I am to take you, madam, to pay your respects to the princess, just as soon as you are well enough.'

Mary cringed. So they were keeping this up! They were still pretending that she wasn't a princess. How long could this last?

'I am *not* well enough,' she said, through gritted teeth. 'I am ill.' She wanted something to eat, but felt it was too humiliating to have to ask.

He bowed again, and looked blank, as if there was nothing further to say.

Mary silently closed the door, and stood thinking for a second. There was nothing for it. She got into the bed and pulled up all the blankets. Here, surely, she would warm up. Here, surely, she could fall asleep, and maybe this horrible dream would be over.

Try as she might, Mary couldn't think how she could have avoided it. But it had been a terrible mistake to come here to Hatfield.

Chapter 11

December 1533, Hatfield

The next morning, it was exactly the same. Mary opened the door to find that she was still guarded. This time it was a different servant outside, a serving man of lower rank than the household gentleman of yesterday.

When he saw the movement in the doorway, he stood smartly to attention and whisked off his woollen cap. Mary knew, by observing him through a very narrow crack, that he had been amusing himself for the last quarter-hour with his knife, throwing it into the floorboards and trying to hit the same spot twice.

Again, just like last night, he offered to take her to 'the princess'. Again, she refused.

'I don't understand you,' she said shortly. 'I am the princess.' She knew she didn't look like it, wan, dishevelled, with no water to wash in nor clean linen to wear. But she was desperate enough to ask for some food.

'You wish to eat?' he asked quickly. 'I shall conduct you down to our lord and our lady Shelton. They are breaking their fast just now, I believe.'

'No, no, I am not well enough for that,' Mary said. 'I must eat here in my room. Pray send some broth and some bread. Food for an invalid.'

He bowed but did not leave.

'Please,' she said. She was so hungry that she was almost ready to whimper.

'Madam,' he said, looking shiftily at the ground, 'I have been told not to leave your door unguarded. I am told to accompany you if you wish to go to Sir John or her ladyship, or to the princess, but otherwise, I am to bid you keep to your room. Until my fellow comes to relieve me.'

Mary winced. So she was a prisoner! In effect, at least, she was trapped. She realised Sir John and Lady Shelton's plan: to keep her up here, in this room, unless she did what she was determined not to do, which was to go to see her baby half-sister. If she once kissed her sister's hand, or curtseyed, or addressed the baby as 'Princess', Mary would be acknowledging that she had been ousted from the royal family. She understood it. That's what they were trying to achieve.

But she was not sure that the serving man understood it, for his face was troubled.

He nearly spoke, but then there was the sound of footsteps coming along the gallery. Mary's heart leapt. Had someone come to help her?

Looking out through the door, she saw it was the serving woman she remembered from last night. The woman was bustling along with a lacquered tray in her hands. On it Mary could glimpse bread, and was that faint steam escaping from a tankard? It was certainly cold enough, in this draughty top floor of the great wooden house, for a warm drink to produce steam.

Mary's stomach growled loudly. Yes, it was food, and it was for her.

Nodding at the man but not at all slowing her pace, the grey-clad woman was heading right in through the door. He seemed uncertain, for a moment, about whether he should stop her, but it was too late. Mary opened the door fully, stepped aside, and closed it smartly after the woman with the tray.

The serving woman put her burden down on the linen chest, having looked around the room for a moment in search of something more suitable. Mary looked longingly at the tray. But she guessed that this woman was more important to her than the food. She quietly placed her hand on the servant's shoulder and whispered in her ear.

'Who are you?'

The woman smiled, and beckoned Mary into the corner by the window.

'If we whisper,' she hissed, 'I hope he won't hear us.' Mary understood that she meant the man outside. Mary started to speak, but the woman used her hand to make a quick gesture.

'I am so sorry, Your Royal Highness,' she whispered. 'But time is short. My name is Clem. If I stay and talk, I will be missed. There is something I must say to you. Look at your tray carefully. I will come later, to take it away, and I will also take away your message. I cannot get you writing materials. You must *tell* me what message you want to send. I will remember it. And keep it short. It is dangerous!'

Then before Mary could answer, she was bustling away, out of the door, calling out cheerfully to the servant. 'Some buttered ale for you, Stephen?' she asked. 'When I come back up for the tray?'

Mary could hear him respond, pleased, and the burble of their conversation continued for a minute or two.

She was surprised. Royal servants would never have allowed themselves to disturb the ears of their betters in this manner. But these weren't really royal servants yet, it was clear. They had felt sorry for her last night, and they had shown it. They were the newly assembled household of a baby princess, not yet fully trained, nor able to predict the wishes of their lord and lady.

However, listening to Clem's conversation with the man outside in the gallery about ale, and the weather, and how cold it was for the time of year, wasn't Mary's priority. The tray! What was significant about the tray?

She almost ran to the linen chest. Yes, here was a pewter plate, with bread on it, and a cup. It was warm ale, with butter mixed in. Mary's empty stomach wanted to drink it all at once. She was so thirsty! The bread didn't look so good. It had a nasty hard crust, and the pewter looked … well, dirty, after the silver salvers she was used to. But the ale could wait. What else was here? She carefully lifted the cup off the plate, examining it. Nothing. She picked up the bread. Nothing. Then she lifted the pewter dish itself. There! Underneath was the tiniest square of parchment, folded very tight.

It wasn't sealed, and Mary's fingers, although they were cold and clumsy, undid it in a trice.

She looked at the door, aware that it wasn't locked, and that the man outside could come in at any moment. She'd been pleased that they hadn't locked her in, but now she regretted being unable to lock people out.

Mary stood with her back against the door, so that if he tried to open it, it wouldn't budge. She was also ready to scrunch up the letter in a flash if she felt even the slightest pressure against her shoulder blades.

Instantly, her eye recognised her mother's hand. She felt almost a physical pleasure, like someone giving her a hug. She had been remembered! Her mother had remembered her!

The letter did not begin with Mary's name, which was odd. But then Mary realised that this was perhaps sensible. If people, if that serving woman Clem, had run risks to get it to her, then it was best kept brief and plain.

I have heard such tidings, her mother's handwriting told her, *that tell me the time when Almighty God will test you is very near. They will press you. Answer with few words. Say you will obey the orders of your father, the king, in everything, save only that you will not offend God. Remember I love you.*

Mary's knees slowly gave way, and her back slid down the door until her legs were out straight ahead of her on the floor.

This was treason. Sending this letter was treason. Her mother was risking everything to have sent it, and her request therefore had the force of a command. Yes, Mary must become like one of the martyrs of the Church. She must obey the orders of men as far as she could, but she must not offend God.

She decided on her reply. It would be very short, very safe to deliver. It would simply be: 'yes'.

Of course.

She would continue to resist. She wondered what to do with the letter, how to hide it. The answer came from her stomach. She tore off a little corner, popped it into her mouth, chewed it many, many times, and swallowed. It would make an excellent precursor to breakfast.

Chapter 12

New Year, 1534, Hatfield

Mary fell into something of a routine, warily coexisting with the servants of the house. Each morning, they asked her if she would see her sister the princess, but each morning Mary said she was too ill.

The serving woman Clem brought her breakfast. At dinner time, Mary agreed to descend to eat. She and the Sheltons sat in silence at the long table in the Great Hall. Mary rebuffed Sir John's every attempt at conversation; every attempt he made to make her go to pay her respects to her sister. Her eye was often drawn to the figure of Lady Shelton, elegant and thin, usually dressed in black, and always, always silent.

Mary went back to her room after the midday meal and refused to come out again. She always felt hungry in the evenings, but she ate as much as she could at dinner and, of course, every last bite of her breakfast. How she enjoyed her breakfast! It was always the best part of the day.

In her room, Mary spent long hours jumping up on to and down from the linen chest. She was trying to keep some strength in her legs, which were growing useless from want of exercise.

The days went slowly by. On bright mornings, Mary looked out of the window at the sun shining on the frosty grasses below. She had a view of the garden, many, many floors down. It delighted her to see the occasional gardener creeping slowly along the path with his barrow and hoe. It reminded her that the world still contained other people. It was easy to forget this.

Once, one of the manservants outside her door fell asleep on his stool, and Mary could hear the loud, rhythmic hiss of his snores. She thought about leaving the room, even if only to walk up and down the gallery. But there was no point. She wouldn't get far before someone would spot her and ask her if she was going to the Princess Elizabeth. She sat on the floor, though, with her ear against the door, listening to the man snore. There was generally so little to listen to that it almost sounded like music.

Another day, Mary looked down into the garden to see a slow procession of ladies creeping along the path. At their rear came the stately figure of Lady Shelton, all in black and bearing a bundle. Mary could not see exactly what the bundle contained, but she was pretty sure this was her baby half-sister, out for an airing with her household. From the floors below, she would sometimes hear distant laughter, and even singing at night. It was Christmas, after all.

The sight of her sister made Mary lonelier than ever. She now felt that she had been wicked, in the crowded days of her old life at Greenwich, to wish that she could more often be alone. Now she was alone all the time, and she didn't like it. Mary squeezed the front of her stays together, there to hear the rustle of her mother's latest letter. She had not eaten it yet, as she wanted to read it again. She rather wished that it had said more about what her mother was doing, and less about God.

But then, if her mother was likewise being held in a grand prison, just as Mary was, she was probably doing nothing. Just as Mary was.

As the New Year turned, Mary prayed to God for something to change. She knew that her father would be celebrating at Greenwich, and wished he wanted her there by his side, as she had been last year. She had been at Hatfield for weeks now. How long could it last? Even her clothes, as well as her nerves, were wearing out. Her dress had not been cleaned or brushed at all, and her linen was taken from her to be washed just once a week.

In January, something happened at last. Mary's ear was finely attuned to the sounds of the household, and she could tell that something was afoot.

There was more noise than usual down below, and when her breakfast came it was brought by an unknown serving man, not the friendly Clem.

Mary tried to damp down her hopes. Perhaps something awful had at last happened to the wicked Lady Anne. But it could equally well be bad news.

Perhaps Lady Anne – for surely it was her, not Mary's father, who had ordered her to be kept prisoner – had got impatient. Perhaps Lady Anne had sent the Duke of Norfolk to take Mary to the Tower of London.

If that was the case, Mary thought, squaring up her chin, then so be it. It would be what God, her mother's good but demanding God, wanted.

Thank goodness it was only two days since her linen had been washed. Mary did the best she could to get ready, to look like the princess she was. She used her napkin and the water jug to clean her face and hands, and she picked up the tiny ivory comb Clem had given her. It was impossible for Mary without help to plait or arrange her hair as in the old days at court, so she just combed it long and loose.

But Mary was still dissatisfied with her preparations. If it *was* the Duke of Norfolk, or an important visitor from court, she needed to be able to express, through her appearance alone, how ill she had been treated. How could she signal that the Sheltons had scarcely let her leave her chamber?

An idea came to her. Was it still here? Yes, the knife that had one day been left on the breakfast tray was still under the mattress of her bed. She ferreted it out. She lifted up a great hank of her hair and sliced. It was hard to cut, but the action was satisfying. She began to saw faster and faster, so much so that her arm ached. A pile of brown hair began to build upon the coverlet of the bed.

Yes! Even if they did not let her speak, then this would be a silent protest that something wrong, very wrong, had been done to her.

Mary left off her cap and fluffed up the short ends of her hair. It felt soft, unusual, like the fur of an animal.

At midday, the usual heavy step came along the gallery. Mary braced herself. The usual respectful tap.

'Dinner, my Lady Mary?'

She opened the door immediately and came out quickly, pushing past Sir John before he could stop her. She walked ahead of him along the gallery, imagining that she was at Greenwich, finely dressed, all ready to face the courtiers and ambassadors of Europe, as she had done so often before. It felt a little draughty round the back of her neck, but Mary imagined that she was wearing her hair up, like her mother, under a hood.

She could tell that Sir John was displeased.

'What, has something happened?' he was asking as he tried to keep up with her. 'Have you injured your head?'

'What is that, Sir John?' she said distantly, over her shoulder, pretending that she had not heard.

'This is most unfortunate,' he said.

Mary half smiled as she realised that he wasn't quite sure what she had done, and knew only that she looked different.

'Has someone come to the house?' Mary asked, bounding ahead down the staircase and quickly passing her sister's floor before he could go through the usual rigmarole of insisting that she go there to pay her respects.

He didn't answer.

'My wife will be most displeased,' he was saying. 'Your appearance. Your sister …'

But Mary was already at the bottom of the stairs, and entering the Great Hall.

There she saw the very last person she wanted to see. There, by the fire, was the woman who was now Mary's stepmother. Her enemy.

Mary noticed that Lady Shelton was standing nearby, presumably just having handed the lady the neatly swaddled little sausage of baby that lay in Anne Boleyn's arms.

Mary also noticed, with satisfaction, Lady Shelton's start of surprise at seeing her shorn hair. But Mary also experienced a curious feeling about the sight of the baby sausage. This tiny girl, too, was her enemy. Yet how could such a small thing hurt Mary? She would rather have liked to have looked at her sister closely, maybe stroked her little pink cheek.

The lady looked up. Mary remembered, though it seemed extraordinary, that the court now called her Queen Anne.

'Ah,' Anne said, without preamble. 'Lady Shelton has been telling me that you have still refused to pay my daughter the respect that is fitting from a servant to a mistress. You are a servant now, do you hear?'

Mary knew that she looked like one, with her ragged hair, her drab black dress. But she stood up straight.

'I respect my father, the king, and my mother, the queen,' she said. 'I respect God. But I did not ask to come here, and I do not respect those who keep me here against my will.'

There was something like a snarl from Lady Shelton.

But Anne was more than equal to Mary's defiance.

'You mention God,' she said smoothly. 'Let us begin there. You think you obey God's will? For your father is head of the Church, you know, and it is *his* will that you accept your sister as your superior.'

'I do not accept that my father is head of the Church. That is the Pope in Rome. My father only created his own new church because the true Church rightly said it was illegal for him to set my mother aside.'

It was hard to speak without trembling, with the lady sitting before her, looking so relaxed and comfortable, her baby upon her knee. Mary braced herself to endure the murmur of disapproval that arose from the other ladies, around and behind Lady Shelton. They clearly thought that punishment would be coming Mary's way.

'I think that God would want you to honour your father and king,' Anne said. 'And I see you have fallen into the dangerous heresy that the Bishop of Rome has any power in this land of England. He has none, you know, Mary. And we sensible modern people don't need the flummery and magic of the old ways.'

'The old ways, as you call them,' Mary said, 'the old ways of my mother's and my own religion, gave us many wise monks and holy nuns, and many hospitals, and charities, and chantries, and books of wisdom.'

'Superstition,' said the lady sadly, looking down at the baby sausage. 'They gave us ignorance, and darkness, and superstition.'

'Charity,' Mary said. 'Kindness.'

There was a long pause.

'Ah, but I will not argue with you,' Anne said. 'Your mother always bested your father in matters of logic, in the old days, when she was failing in so many other ways as queen. Actions, Mary, speak louder than words. And if you will not respect your sister, if you will not respect me …'

Mary had not curtseyed upon entering the room – it had not occurred to her to do so – but clearly that had rankled.

'… then we must repay you in kind. My aunt tells me that you are not well enough to eat with your sister's household, and that you have breakfast in your own chamber. That will stop, you know. That will stop until you are ready to do your duty, to God, to your father, to your sister. You will never win.'

'Ah,' said Mary. 'But I thought you said my mother *always* won arguments?'

There was a pause.

'Adieu, Mary!' Anne said, waving her away.

Mary closed her eyes. Good Lord, Anne was so confident that she really did not feel the need to argue.

'May God open your eyes,' the lady continued, displaying her uncanny talent for observation, for she sat many feet distant from Mary. 'And may your own dirty God fill your stomach, for it is sure that this household will not.'

Mary was trembling with the effort of keeping herself together. She almost failed when the murmur of the women turned to approbation at the lady's words, and clucks of agreement. She found Sir John at her elbow, and under the pressure of his hand she returned to the staircase. She would not stoop to a physical struggle.

She could smell soup, and roasting meat, and she was hungry. But she was far too tense to worry about that.

Mary knew she had just endured another round in the fight to the death. But although she had scored a few points, it hadn't been much of a victory.

Chapter 13

January 1534, Hatfield

Three days later, Mary was feeling grim. Now the little panelled room off the gallery sometimes seemed to blur and spin before her eyes. Her faculties were refusing to work properly. She could feel her shrinking stomach pulling her flesh, even the flesh of her face, downwards and inwards, towards itself. She was tensing and tightening up like the dried skin of a snake.

Three days. She could not have failed to count them. The lady must have left Hatfield after having visited her daughter, for the household seemed to return to normal. Mary had not been downstairs; in fact, she had not been out of her room. Each morning, she was asked if she was well enough to pay her respects to her sister the princess.

And when she said she was not, the door was shut abruptly in her face.

And now, with no need for breakfast trays, it was harder for Clem to bring her letters. One had arrived in her chamber pot. It seemed that Mary's mother's spies had not had the chance to pass on the news of the commandment that Mary would have no food. The chamber pot letter, as usual, had ordered her to be firm and to trust God. Reading it, Mary wondered that God should want anything to do with her, with her tufty hair, her shrunken face, and her black dress that was growing a little ragged as well as rusty with wear. She had it on all day and sometimes, if the night was cold, as it often was, all night as well.

On the fourth day, Mary was sipping some water, and trying to remember what it was like to have a head that didn't ache, when she noticed something unusual. Yes, there was that extra dimension to the sounds coming from the floors below, more of them, more varied, just as there had been when the wicked lady visited.

Perhaps Anne Boleyn was back again, to see whether starvation had changed Mary's mind. The thought made her stomach heave up into a sort of horrible dry retch.

Towards the dinner hour, she heard the manservant outside her door lumbering to his feet from his stool, and she heard the cheery 'halloa!' which Clem always let out as she entered the gallery outside Mary's room. Clem! Was Clem bringing food?

But perhaps … what was this? … was Clem taking over as her guard? Yes, clearly this was the case. Mary, leaning against the door panel, was glued to the conversation. She heard it all clearly: the king had arrived, there was an urgent need for more manservants downstairs, he was to go down, Clem was to replace him.

Mary's heart beat fast. Her father was here! In this very house! Mary almost panted with relief. Surely her father would let her have something to eat.

But then doubt entered her mind. How far was he still under the influence of Anne Boleyn's dark doe eyes? Had Anne persuaded Mary's father that his daughter was disobedient?

That was ridiculous, Mary told herself sternly. A surge of confidence, faith in her father's love, rushed through her. He had once tossed her joyfully in the air. He had once called her his Mighty Princess. His horrible so-called wife must be hoping he wouldn't discover that Mary was here, locked away like this.

How to let him know?

She got to her feet, trembling. It would be difficult, she was sure of that. Anne Boleyn and the Sheltons would not want their cruelty to be detected.

She almost fell as the door was suddenly shoved towards her. Clem had opened it, and Mary's legs were too weak to brace themselves properly.

As usual, Clem didn't waste time.

'Quick!' she said. 'This is your chance. I have not been given the duty of guarding the door before. I can tell them I did not know how to do it properly, and that you took me by surprise. Go down the stairs, very fast. The first floor above the ground, that's where he is. He's in the princess's Great Chamber. When he sees you – Lord, when anyone sees you – he will know how bad things are.'

Mary paused a second. 'But Clem, will you not get into trouble?'

Clem was her only friend in this place. Mary could not afford to lose her.

Clem looked grim. 'Go, for your mother's sake and for the sake of our religion.'

This did the trick. Other people, not just Mary herself, needed her to be strong.

She set off along the gallery as best as she could. Her steps were uneven, and the pain in her hollow stomach kept her bent over forward. The stairs! Here were the stairs. She almost slipped, and found she had to shuffle down, one step at a time. Quickly. Quietly.

There was a definite buzz in the atmosphere, the sound of horses in the courtyard below, and voices, and indeed the distant clang of cooking pots.

One by one, Mary slithered her way down the steps of the staircase. Her heart lurched into her mouth as she passed the landing of the third floor, for she heard the footsteps of other people in the passage beyond. Then she was descending to the second floor, the most important floor, where her baby sister lived. The hammering of her heart seemed to fill her ears. Which way, which way to the princess's Great Chamber? She wished she knew more about the geography of this part of the house, to which she had never been.

Right, she decided. Turn right. As the most important room, her sister's Great Chamber was probably towards the middle of the house rather than the end.

Mary was off the stairs now and into a wide passage, and yes. Ahead, past several other doorways, she could see into an illuminated room. That certainly was the Great Chamber! All lit with candles, because although it was midday, the January sun seemed to have scarcely any power.

Mary was drawn irresistibly towards the glow. It was a strange, compelling vision of her old life, before she had to wear only black and starve in a garret. She could see rich hangings, and a chair, oh yes, a velvet chair with crossed legs as her mother and father and even she had once had, in her private chambers at Greenwich.

And then, she heard hear her father's booming laugh.

A little smile crossed Mary's face. Relief filled her. As soon as he saw her sallow, pitiful, distressed state, he would know. He would cast aside his so-called wife, and return Mary to her rightful place.

Unfortunately, so unfortunately, a slender, elegant figure now crossed between Mary and the light and colour within the doorway. Even at this distance, Mary could glimpse the rich purple of a gown. Mary could tell, all too well, that it was Anne, and that Mary herself had been spotted. Anne must have been crossing the room to fetch something; perhaps Mary's movement in the passage had caught her eye.

Mary shrank back against the passage wall, praying to remain unseen, but she could see the silhouetted oval of the lady's face turned towards her. It was too dark to make out the individual features, but she knew, just knew, that those black eyes were staring at her. Should she cry out? Would her father hear?

It was too late. Men were coming out of the Great Chamber now, large men, moving quickly, and its door was slamming hard. Yes, here was Sir John

Shelton, and another man, and now they each had one of Mary's arms, and now they were dragging her along the passage and back up the stairs.

She did not have the strength to resist. She felt like a rag doll being carried along, with no energy to do anything but almost revel in her own disappointment. So near! She had been so near to letting her father know that she was a prisoner!

At the top of the stairs, Sir John shoved her into the gallery, before banging and locking its door behind her. Mary crouched on the floor and gradually tried to recover herself. Her throat seemed to retch all by itself. Her whole body had been unpleasantly started by the quick action they had forced upon her in her weakness, and she felt terribly dizzy.

She noticed the fine wide wooden floorboards of the gallery beneath her hands. They had not bothered to take her to her room, then. Presumably she was locked in, locked into this whole floor, because all the servants were needed below. Mary could see that this was a quick and easy solution to the problem she presented.

Mary lay on the floor for several minutes, bitter waves of disappointment pinning her down. A tear of frustration ran sideways down her cheek. Quickly she used her finger to carry it to her tongue, relishing its salty taste. She could not afford to waste her tears.

At last, gathering all her strength, Mary heaved herself to a sitting position. She knew that she must explore the opportunity that she now had. What else was on this floor apart from her own room, and the long gallery itself, with its now-empty stool for her absent guard? Clem had disappeared, and Mary hoped that she would not be punished for Mary's escape.

She half walked, half slid along the gallery to her own room. Inside it, she found a pleasant surprise. There was bread! A great roll of bread, bigger than her hand, was lying on the bed. Clem must have left it there for her. Mary was torn between devouring it like a wolf, and making the most of her semi-freedom. The bread won. It was soon in her mouth. She had to force herself to chew it rather than swallow it whole. Plain, dry bread, but more delicious than any banquet she'd ever eaten. At once she felt a little strength returning to her limbs.

Mary was staring round her own little chamber, seeing it anew, and suddenly wondered if it had a matching equivalent at the other end of the gallery.

She crept back along the gallery again. Yes, here at the far end was a door. It led not to a room, like Mary's, but to a little staircase winding upwards. Mary climbed it, anxious, excited. The stairs were dusty, and she felt the trailing back of her dress picking up salty flakes of stone. But this was far too important to care.

At the top, another door, which opened easily under her hands. Here was the roof! She was out on the roof!

Mary stepped forward into the cold air, and crept down the roof slope towards the carved balustrade. An immense view made her sway: the courtyard, full of horses, the park beyond, the roofs of the houses of the village, and above all, the white sky. She had not seen the sky for many weeks. It was so big, so bright. It almost crushed her.

But Mary knew that she could not afford to enjoy

the sky. Something was happening below. Yes, the horses were lining up and forming a cavalcade, and that large bright figure now coming down the steps, and towards a fine black horse, that was, that was …

'Father!'

Mary thought she screamed the word. But it came out like a little squeak.

She filled her lungs to try again.

'Father! Father!'

She frantically waved her arms. She whirred them like a windmill.

'Father! Father! Father!'

It was no good. Mary's heart sank. They hadn't heard her. There was too much going on in the courtyard, with the mounting of the riders, and she knew all too well how the king drew everyone's eyes.

She'd try just once more. Gathering all her strength and all her spirit, Mary made a frantic final yell.

And it worked.

Maybe the wind changed, maybe by chance a

hush fell over the men and horses gathered below, but someone saw her. Eyes were shaded by hands. People were turning. Yes, her father was turning, and looking, and wondering what was going on.

She could sense the consternation among the servants, the panic that set in when any royal arrangement went slightly awry. A jolt of pleasure ran through her. Yes, they had seen her. Here she was, outlined against the sky, with her sadly shorn hair and her black dress. Yes, they could see, *they knew*, how the Princess Mary had been treated.

And best of all, her father was now looking up at her. She could see his broad face beneath his up-tilted hat, his characteristic stance with his legs planted wide apart.

Mary smiled.

'*Father*,' she whispered, one more time.

But then, to her utter horror, she realised that someone else was coming into that same sector of courtyard. There was the groom holding her father's horse, head bowed, respectfully awaiting orders. And there *she* was, flying down the steps, and crossing over to him at a light run, and grasping his arm, and speaking urgently into his ear.

Mary knew that his eyes were looking at her. She stared back intently. *Don't turn away*, she willed. *See me! Don't turn away.*

But it was too late. Whatever poison Anne was pouring into his ear, it was working. He did not appear indignant or angry. He seemed uncertain and embarrassed. Eventually, the lady, her harangue finished, stepped aside.

There was another pause, her father standing and looking up at Mary for a long moment. At that distance, Mary could not see exactly what expression was on his face, but she had no doubt that he recognised her, and knew that he was looking at his daughter.

And then finally he stepped forward, raised his hat to her, and turned. He was getting on to his horse; he was riding away.

Chapter 14

February 1534, Hatfield

Mary is eighteen …

It was betrayal, there was no doubt about that. Mary's own father had turned against her. It was a bitter, bitter blow, and each time she recalled the sight of him raising his hat it made her feel even sicker than she already was.

But in some ways, things were clearer. She was no longer suspended between fear and hope. Anne had completely turned her father. It must be true, after all, as her mother had always said, that her father was in some ways a weak man.

The Sheltons had obviously decided that it was easier to lock Mary into the whole gallery floor than it was to keep her in her room, where they had to trust to a revolving series of household servants to keep her safely inside.

The downside of the new regime was that Mary was now definitely ill. She regretted devouring that loaf on the day of her father's visit, for it had made her belly swell up painfully. And when her belly went down again she was left hungrier than ever. She should have eked the bread out over the coming days.

The one thing they did bring her was water, a jug of it each day, and her chamber pot.

After seeing her father, Mary spent a couple of days lying in her little bed and feeling as low as humanly possible. But eventually she decided that she must try to stay alive. She hated to think what news of her death – for she had begun to think often about dying – might do to her mother.

Having made her decision, Mary slipped out of her own room and along the gallery.

She didn't have anything as firm as a plan, but she wanted to go back up on to the roof, just to see what she could see. She gasped as she opened the door because a freezing wind hit her in the face.

The weather had turned hard and bright. She felt so weak that she did not trust herself to go near the edge, as she had before, to look down into the courtyard.

But the chilly temperature enlivened her, and Mary could feel the blood beginning to pulse through her cheeks. She decided to look at the view the other way, behind the house, where the clipped hedges of the garden gave way to the rough grass of the park.

As she made her slow, slippery way out from behind one of the chimneys, a dreadful sharp crack made her leap out of her skin.

'Hail Mary, full of grace,' Mary whispered, shrinking back at once into the shelter of the chimney stack.

It was a missile of some kind, which had struck the bricks of the chimney and almost hit her. She saw it now, skittering down the leaden slope of the roof towards the balustrade. Yes, an arrow!

Mary stood, her back to the chimney, eyes closed, heart beating fast. Someone had tried to kill her. She wasn't safe. She should have stayed in her room.

But how could she get back to safety without making herself a target once again? There must be a man, or men, with a crossbow in the park, aiming at her. Another whizz. Another arrow. The air was full of death.

Mary stood where she was, eyes closed, praying as hard as she could that the arrows might miss. She had thought death would come slowly, from hunger, not quickly at the hands of an assassin. Suddenly, and very sharply, she wanted to live.

She opened her eyes. From where she stood, she could see the two arrows in the gutter at the edge of the roof. Even as she watched, there was another powerful hum through the air, and another collision with the chimney. Now there were three of them.

The sight of them made her flinch. These things might have killed her!

But they weren't like any arrows Mary had seen before. They did not seem to be made of wood. Mary would have quite liked to scramble down and examine them, but she did not dare. She stood and waited, getting colder and colder. Eventually, her knees started shaking, and a dreadful shivering wracked her. She grew reckless. She wasn't going to die of cold, no way. She was going to make an end of it.

She made a bolt back for the top of the stairs, without any more arrows being fired.

She spent the afternoon in the gallery feeling nauseous. She shuffled her mattress along so she could lie upon it in a square of uncertain sunlight from the window. When the sun went down, Mary grew deadly cold.

She decided to move. Back to the roof. Those arrows had been puzzling her.

It was a slow climb up. She had to pause every so often on the stairs through dizziness. Then came a cold slither across the leads, to find the three arrows, now almost invisible in the dark.

Yes, once they were in her hand, there was definitely something odd about the arrows, their shafts felt ... soft. They were not like any arrows she had seen before, because round each wooden shaft something else was wrapped. Mary's heart beat faster. Was this a message? Was this how her mother's spies would communicate with her now that Clem was no longer allowed to bring her food?

It wasn't paper, though, it was … a long strip of dried bacon. Each one! Yes, three long strips of meat! She smelt it. Oh, but the ham smelt good. Mary cursed herself for misunderstanding the arrows earlier. They hadn't been sent to kill her, but to bring her life. This meat, oh, but it was chewy, and salty, and delicious, and it was going to save her soul.

She carefully ate just one of the pieces, saving the rest. Slowly, savouring each mouthful, she began to feel just a little bit better. Even better than food, though, was the thought that she had not been forgotten. Deep down, she believed, she *knew*, that her mother was behind this.

Chapter 15

February 1534, Hatfield

There had been no need to hoard the meat. The next day, three more arrows. Three more meals of dried ham. Mary began to feel a little strength returning. She tried to spend the day exercising, moving up and down the gallery. The sun became very important to her. She loved it and revelled in it when it shone, and mourned it when it did not.

Sometimes, when she was feeling delirious, and when the sun moved on to her featherbed, she almost imagined that she could hear an angel talking to her, telling her that her mother was alive and well, and worrying about her. But then, when the sun slipped back behind a cloud, the angel seemed to be saying that Mary's mother was taking her love away again. Mary had not pleased God. Mary had not yet become one of his martyrs.

Each evening, the gallery door was unlocked, very briefly, and fresh water delivered. Once Mary had been sleeping in her room and hadn't noticed.

But usually there was a sharp knocking to alert her, then the scraping of the lock, then Sir John, accompanied by one or two stern servants, appeared, asking her, always, if she was ready now to go to her sister and name her as princess.

Quietly, respectfully, Mary refused. She tried to look as weak as possible at these meetings, so that he would not suspect that her mother's spies were succeeding in getting her food.

Then, one day, Mary was not sure how many days later, it wasn't just Sir John at the door. It was a strange man in rich furs, with a jowly face, and with two drab manservants standing behind him. Mary hadn't seen either him or them before at Hatfield.

When he saw her, he gasped.

'But this is not right!'

His voice. His voice wasn't right either. Who was

he? Those rich clothes, the servants, and yet he sounded like a mean man of the streets. It was confusing.

Despite the meat, Mary was still feeling headachy and sick. She was surprised and frightened by the change in the routine. She knew that she ought to appear weak, but there was no acting involved when she collapsed to the ground as her legs gave way.

In a trice, the man was leaning over her, full of concern. It was hard for him to crouch with his great bulk, but he did so with alacrity.

'Quick!' he was calling to his men. 'Fetch some fiery spirits! She has fainted. And she's cold! Can you stand? Can you stand if I help you? You must come down to the fire at once.'

Mary's eyes were not working properly, her head was spinning, but she sensed that she was lolling weakly in his arms. The three men half carried her from the gallery, down the grand stairs, and into a chamber.

Mary felt, though, that she was travelling up, up towards heaven, and that the Virgin Mary was once again smiling at her in welcome. From far, far away, she sensed a voice calling urgently to her. It grew louder.

'Come back to us! Come back!'

It was the strange jowly man, his face now lit by flickering firelight. Mary took possession once again of her actual body, her useless, aching limbs, and her pounding horrible head. Slowly, she found the strength to move her eyes.

Mary wasn't sure where in the house she was, and she hadn't seen this room before. It had beautiful tapestries, a sight she'd almost forgotten and … a fire, yes, a roaring, blazing fire. He placed a woolly sheepskin on a chair by the hearth, and Mary was sitting in it. Now a cup containing something warm was being put into her hands, but she lacked the strength to hold it.

'Here,' he said gently, as if coaxing a very young child, and lifted it to her lips.

She sipped it, and the taste and richness of it almost knocked her out. 'They have been mistreating you,' he said sadly. 'I see it. I wish I had come sooner.'

Mary looked up, the hot, winey drink starting to

revive her. Caudle, it was hot caudle. There were currants in it. It was the most delicious thing she had ever drunk.

'Do you come from my mother?' she said eagerly.

Almost at once she wished she had not spoken. If he *didn't* come from her mother, she might be revealing secrets. Mary realised, too late, that he hadn't called her 'Princess'. If he came from her mother, then surely he would have done so.

He laughed.

'Oh, no,' he said. He was distracted by a sound, by someone coming to the door. Mary heard him telling whoever it was that he was not to be disturbed.

Then he came back, and sat opposite her.

'Cake,' he said. She now saw a spread of figgy pudding and gingerbread on a silver dish at her elbow. Carefully, she ate a little. She was on guard now, as well as not wanting to overexert her belly too soon. But God alone knew how good the sweet food was.

'I've come from your father. My name is Thomas Cromwell.'

Mary paused in the very act of chewing. She didn't know what to think.

'Your father,' he said, 'would be horrified, horrified, to know what has been happening here at Hatfield.'

Mary bit back the response that her father had seen it for himself. He had seen her, desperate, up on the roof. And he had done nothing.

'His servants,' Cromwell went on, 'are sometimes too zealous in his name. The king of course cannot see to everything personally. His servants sometimes overstep the mark in doing what they *think* he wants them to do. It is quite wrong that the daughter of the king has been kept in this manner. I have arranged at once for your own servants and proper clothes to be restored to you.'

Mary thought this was rather missing the point.

'My *meals*,' she explained. 'Most of all I need to eat. Without harassment.'

'Yes, yes, the Sheltons have been most neglectful.'

'*Cruel!*' Mary said angrily. 'It's not neglect, they have been deliberately cruel to me!'

'You are right,' he said sadly. 'They have over-stepped, most grievously. But this is better, is it not?'

Mary looked around the warm, fire-lit room, and nodded. There was a bed in its shadows, with proper curtains, and she could see a blue blanket. And was that a heap of fresh linen laid upon it? Clean clothes?

'Is this …' She hardly dared hope. 'Is this to be my room?'

'Most certainly!' he said reassuringly. 'You are of royal blood, and you deserve the comforts and state of that condition. You won't be returning to that miserable gallery.'

'But if that is true, then I wish to leave Hatfield!'

Mary's heart leapt. Her father had rescued her! Her father had sent this man, at last, to rectify the terrible wrong, to treat her as she deserved, and in no time she would be gone from here. Oh, how wrong she had been to lose faith in him. She would insist on leaving now, today. She grasped the arm of the chair in preparation for an attempt to stand.

For a second she felt a pang of regret that someone had worked so hard to get this lovely room ready for her, when she would never sleep a night in it.

'Ah, my lady,' Master Cromwell said, in his quiet, sad voice. 'I'm afraid that can't happen. You must stay at Hatfield, you know, until your sister the princess leaves it. And all you need do to maintain a comfortable way of living, and clothes, and food ...'

He nodded at the plate of gingerbread, which was by now almost empty.

'All you need to do is sign this one little piece of paper. Then everyone will leave you alone. You won't have to do anything else.'

'What is it?' Mary asked suspiciously. She felt drained and empty. This wasn't rescue after all. It was just some new tactic.

'It's just a paper that says that you will submit to the Act of Succession, that's all. It's the Act of Parliament, you know, the will of the people, which outlines the inheritance of the throne. From your father, to your sister, and then to you.'

'It should be me before my sister,' Mary said dully.

'Just one little signature,' he wheedled.

'No,' Mary said.

'So easy!'

It did look easy. The firelight flickered over the paper. The inkstand was ready, he was holding out a quill towards her. She saw his face, beseeching, friendly. She did want to please him.

'No!' she said. Some explanation, she felt, was necessary. 'My mother,' she said weakly. She tensed herself for what was next.

There was silence. He said nothing, but sighed.

'Am I to go ... back upstairs?' she asked meekly.

'No, no!' he said. 'Oh, I see you didn't understand,' he continued. 'From now on, I will look after you. Eventually, I know, you will come to sign. Now, I think you need sleep, my dear.'

He rose, and left Mary sitting by her fire, in her tapestried room, with her gingerbread, and her delicious-looking bed waiting. But she felt horribly uneasy.

Chapter 16

February 1534, Hatfield

By morning, Mary felt even more troubled. She couldn't get comfortable in her bed. It was too soft, too warm. She wasn't used to it. And the gingerbread *had* disordered her stomach. She had a dull pain down there.

She fell asleep, deeply, just before dawn. Mary came out of her sleep with brutal suddenness when a scraping noise jarred her ears. A bright shaft of sun was coming through the high, latticed window, and was making the colours of the tapestry glow.

As Mary blinked, attempting to get her eyes to focus, she saw a tall figure in black, poker in hand, crossing from the window to the fire, and beginning to stir it into new life.

A tall figure, a well-tailored figure … a horrible jolt ran through Mary's body. But then, looking more closely, Mary realised that it wasn't the wicked lady, but her aunt. Lady Shelton.

This was indeed a new stratagem. Mary was still on guard. What did Lady Shelton want? Before, Mary had been taken into the presence of Lady Shelton, just as ambassadors went before the king. Now Lady Shelton sensed that she was being watched, turned, and came towards Mary, just as if she were the supplicant. Her eyebrows, black and arched and horribly like her niece Anne's, were raised in polite enquiry.

'Good morning, my lady,' said Lady Shelton. 'Did you sleep well? Your breakfast will be here very shortly. A little hot porridge, perhaps? It's cold again this morning.'

Her voice, which Mary had never heard before, was surprisingly deep and low.

Despite having come out of her sleep so short a time ago, Mary was wide awake. She had so many questions that she wanted to ask. If she ate the food, would they … *make* her sign her rights away? Could they do that? Did they intend to relax her, make her lower her guard?

'Thank you,' she said shortly, at last.

Perhaps it was best to say as little as may be. She longed for her mother's advice. She had not received a letter, nor seen Clem for, oh, weeks now.

Lady Shelton was curtseying – yes, actually curtseying! – and backing towards the door. It was a strange feeling. It had been so long since anyone had paid Mary the ceremonies of her status that she'd almost forgotten what it was like. *Perhaps*, she thought, *I'm only a princess when other people think that I am.* Then she imagined her mother's scornful reaction to such a statement, and almost laughed out loud. Yes, of course, her mother would say that Mary had the very blood of a princess, and would always be one.

Mary was left alone to enjoy the sunlight, and the bright clean fire. In due course, serving women – not Clem, but other serving women with reddened hands and clean aprons – brought in hot water, and a beautiful linen shift, almost pure white. And – what was this? – a new gown, plum-coloured velvet with silver embroidery. They held it up, ready for Mary to get into it.

'Where is the chamber woman called Clem?' she asked.

'Gone back to her family, m'lady,' one of them said, eyes lowered. 'Her sister had a babe. She went to help.'

Thank God! Only just in time, Mary stopped herself from thanking the Lord out loud. So Clem, who had helped her, had escaped!

Feeling lighter at heart, Mary carefully considered the beautiful dress. At length, she shook her head. No, she wasn't going to go that far in embracing this luxurious new lifestyle. She ruefully rubbed her short, spiky hair. She would stick with her old black gown.

A few minutes later, she slightly regretted the decision. Mary realised that in the warmth of the sunlit chamber she could detect a slight stale smell coming off her rusty old black dress. She sighed, rueful for a moment. What did it really matter, though, what she was wearing, if she was stuck in this room? It was still a prison, if more luxurious than her last.

But *was* she stuck? She tried the door. It opened easily, revealing an empty, wide, matted passage. She had not really noticed all this when she was carried along it, half fainting, last night. The windows gave a different view down upon the clipped shapes of the garden, bushes trained into the shapes of ships, and, over to one side, the skeleton of what must, in summer, be a gorgeous green peacock.

After a second or two of looking out, a soft sound made Mary's head whip round sideways. The gallery was not empty after all. Coming along it, towards her, was an elegant young man. He was dressed in black, just as Lady Shelton had been. Mary felt a shiver of disappointment for the rejected plum velvet gown, for here, for the first time in many weeks, was someone her own age.

Suddenly, strangely, she cared what she looked like.

He was smiling now, and trying to bow even though he was carrying a tray. It was odd to see a gentleman carrying a tray. He did it awkwardly, as if he wasn't used to it. Forgetting for a moment whether she was a princess or not, Mary stepped forward to give him a hand.

'Ah, the door, the door,' he said, holding the tray away from her, but playfully. 'If you could kindly open the door. I really am making a mess of this, aren't I?'

Mary lifted the latch, and made as if to lift the heavy jug off the tray to help him.

'No, no!' he said. 'You'll unbalance me. I've learned that much at least between the kitchens and here.'

He was leading the way into Mary's room, putting the tray containing her breakfast down on the table, then rushing around it to fetch a chair for her, eager as a puppy. Mary noticed, as his arms swung about, that his cloak had a lining of silver satin. He really was far too well dressed to be delivering food.

He noticed her noticing him, and stopped, and placed one hand over his heart, and bowed again.

'My Lady Mary,' he said. 'I am Lady Shelton's other nephew.' He stopped, a bit confused. He looked comically to both left and right as if his brain had frozen and he was shaking his head to wake it up again.

'What a clod-head I am,' he said ruefully. 'I mean, the Lady Anne, I mean the queen, is Lady Shelton's niece,' he said. 'She's my cousin. Lady Shelton is both of our ... aunt.'

He was so triumphant at having found the right word for the relationship at last that he smiled, and Mary could not help smiling too.

'So you are Lady Shelton's nephew, that's what you're saying?'

He nodded. Mary realised that if he was the wicked lady's cousin, she ought to hate him. But curiously, his grin was so friendly that it didn't seem to bother her. After all, Mary thought, she had cousins of her own that she'd never even met and didn't know if she liked or not. A person could not be blamed for his or her cousins.

She sat down slowly, wondering what would happen next, and picked up the jug to pour herself a drink. At once he was apologising, and taking it from her.

'Too slow, too slow,' he muttered to himself.

'You're too slow, Reginald. The Lady Mary will sack you at this rate.'

He poured her out a drink, and set it down with a flourish. His enthusiasm was infectious.

'Madam,' he said. 'Have you everything you need?'

Mary thought fast. Yes, she had everything she needed. But the last few minutes had been more entertaining than the whole of the last few weeks. How could she stop him from leaving?

'I might want something,' she said distantly. 'You had better wait.'

He stood by the fire a few steps away, as seemed right for a princess and her gentleman servant, but now he kept up a stream of quips and kind comments and observations that no servant would have dared to make. Mary found herself laughing as he explained how out of place he felt in a household made up of 'twenty-five nursemaids, two milkmaids and a woman highly skilled in the changing of baby nappies'. And he boasted that his horse, Old Humphrey, was one of England's fastest.

'Old Humphrey?' Mary asked. 'He doesn't sound very fast to me.'

'Oh, Old Humphrey goes like a dream,' Reginald reassured her. 'I would like to show you Old Humphrey.'

Mary smiled back, thinking for a second that she would love above all things to see Old Humphrey. Then her smile faded. Of course she could not leave her room.

He noticed. 'You can, you know!' he said encouragingly. 'Master Cromwell's orders. The Lady Mary is to go anywhere, do anything. Just not to leave the estate, not to go beyond the park paling. So you can come to ride! Shall we ride tomorrow, my Lady Mary?'

He knelt down on one knee, humbly, head bowed, in a parody of an obsequious servant. He did it in a way that was funny, not silly.

But Mary had winced when he called her his 'Lady Mary', and he had noticed.

'I can see that it hurts you when … when people use that name,' he said. 'I don't really care what you're called. Perhaps I can just … leave it vague?'

He beseeched her with his eyes, looking up from his ridiculous position on the floor. Mary saw that they were large and warm, like the eyes of a spaniel.

She knew that she should insist on her title, that she was showing weakness, but she simply couldn't make herself objectionable now. She lowered her gaze and began to pick at her bread, rolling little bits of it into balls.

'I think I've everything I need now,' she said at last. 'You may retire, Master Reginald. Yes, I will ride tomorrow.'

He smiled, bowed, tweaked his cloak in the parody of a dandy, and almost danced out of the door. Mary ate the rest of her breakfast eagerly. She might even have said, happily.

Chapter 17

February 1534, Hatfield

Mary spent the rest of the day in her room, preparing herself for a different kind of life. She called back the serving women, and had them bring back the dress she had rejected.

She decided to test the limits of what Reginald said: that nothing was forbidden to her at Hatfield House apart from leaving the estate. So she asked to be brought a bath. It took some time, and she could see that it was not easy at short notice, but eventually clanking pails arrived and Mary was splashing herself in a tub before the fire. She had the serving women comb her hair, and asked them to neaten it.

'I shall fetch Lady Shelton and her embroidery shears,' one of them said.

'Can't you do it yourself?' asked Mary, who did not really want to see Lady Shelton again, particularly not if she were annoyed at being disturbed from some other task about the busy household.

'Please, m'lady,' the serving woman said. 'If I were to hurt you with the blade by accident, it would be the end of my life.'

So Lady Shelton came. After she had finished trimming Mary's clean hair, it felt different, so soft and sleek, almost like the pelt of an otter.

'It's … a becoming look,' said Lady Shelton.

She spoke politely, but Mary could tell it wasn't just an empty phrase. Even peering at her reflection in the murky silver mirror, she could see that having less hair made her white neck look long and curved, like a swan's.

They had brought her many outfits now – a long blue dress fit for a ball, a cloak for riding in black velvet trimmed with mink. Mary asked them to take away the old black-and-brown monstrosity, the smelly shepherd's cloak that she'd worn for many weeks, and burn it.

Then she remembered how it had kept her warm

and alive through some very difficult nights. 'No, wait, don't burn it,' she said quickly. 'Give it to some poor man in the village.' When she had been a proper princess, and lived at court, she'd had no idea what it was like to be cold or hungry. She was determined never to feel like that again if she could help it, but she wouldn't ever forget what it was like.

Lady Shelton gave one of her clipped little nods, as if she approved of Mary's thought. 'Quite right,' she said. 'It is true that your mother always gave a good deal to charity.' Mary was taken aback. Surely Lady Shelton was her mother's enemy? It had been generous of her to mention Catherine, and Mary liked her a little more for having done it.

The next morning, Mary was dressed in a black riding dress and cloak. The serving women apologised for the lack of colour in her outfit, but they explained that it had been hard to find clothes of the right size and make in the neighbourhood, and that this was the only one available.

'Why not just bring me my own from London?' she asked, chagrined. They did not answer, and she realised that for all her new freedoms, it was not as if it were really back to the old days. She sighed. The cloak was almost too hot in this warm room, and she took it off.

Even though the weather was dark and dull compared to yesterday's sunshine, her mood improved when she heard Reginald's step in the passage. She would almost have described it as a prance, especially compared with the heavy trudge of the serving women who moved slowly, deliberately, like beasts of burden. He moved like a thoroughbred. This morning there was no pretence that he was bringing her breakfast; that had been brought, and eaten, and cleared already. He took off his feathered hat, bowed down beautifully low, and then offered her a hand to lead her along the gallery.

'Good morning!' he said. 'Old Humphrey awaits you! And a giddy young palfrey called Mistress Skipsey.'

'Do all the horses here have such ridiculous names?' Mary asked, smiling.

'Are you saying that Old Humphrey is a ridiculous name?' He stopped, and turned to her. 'What impertinence!'

Mary smiled again. He had been deeply impertinent to her, but in such a manner that she'd enjoyed it. No one, apart from her mother, had ever really laughed at her, and it was a joyous feeling, warming her up deep inside. For a moment, she could just pretend to be a normal girl.

They went on together, down the main stairs, and Mary prayed that Master Cromwell was not still lurking around the house. She did not want to see that horrible piece of paper in his hand. And the sight of him would only remind her that her father hadn't sent him to rescue her. It would make her blood boil up, like a pot on the fire, if she were forced to remember yet again how her father had failed to set her free.

The Great Hall was quiet, all the servants busy about their morning's work. When Reginald opened the door, a drift of mist came spilling in. Mary had not realised just how miserable this February morning was, and snuggled the fur more closely around her neck.

'We'll soon warm up as we ride!' he promised her. 'Perhaps a canter. Although I wouldn't like Old

Humphrey to break a leg in the long grass. It's him I'm worried about, of course, not you.'

Then they were breathing in almost as much water as air as they made their way through the fog in the courtyard. Mary could see the white shape of a little horse waiting for her, and she was soon patting its nose. The smell of the horse seemed excitingly pungent after so many weeks indoors. A groom was helping her, and soon she was up, was seated, sideways, on the saddle. She'd wanted to spring on to the horse elegantly and proficiently, but she felt like she was fumbling her way through sheep's wool. She had certainly lost a good deal of strength. While she'd been mounting her horse, she'd been conscious all the time of Reginald, getting on to his own. She could hear him hollering out 'Humps!' and 'Whoa, boy!'

Then they were off, Reginald leading the way, a groom walking alongside to lead Mary's palfrey. She began to relax, to enjoy the feel of the fresh air on her face, to see the sodden foliage, to hear the birds calling. Old Humphrey clearly wanted to pick up the pace, and Mary nodded her permission that

Reginald might ride on, harder, circling back every so often to her and the groom at their stately plod. Once she glanced back, to see the high house looming over them through the mist, but then it was lost to sight. After that she looked only forward, at the white ears of Mistress Skipsey, and at the greys and browns of this beautiful outdoor world.

They travelled out through the park and into woods, passing a lake with wisps of steam arising from its dull green surface. The brambles and bracken were brown and slimy. Reginald, on his taller horse, brushed against a high branch and showered Mary with droplets, but she only laughed. At once he twisted round his broad shoulders, to see if she was all right. When he saw that she was, he smiled.

Eventually they arrived at a park paling, with fields beyond. Reginald dismounted, and held both horses while the groom helped Mary off too. Panting, breathless, she stood in the leaf mould and wondered what he had in mind. Reginald was leading her between the trees, out of earshot of the servant. Mary's heart beat faster. What was going to happen? She felt oddly guilty. The sight of the back of the groom's head, so fixedly turned away from them, had dampened her response to some of Reginald's jokes.

He was taking her to a place where they could get right up against the palings, and Mary saw the fields sloping away into a hollow full of fog. Above it a hazy, glowing ball of sun hovered low on the horizon.

Suddenly she realised what he was showing her.

That was freedom, that sunny field out there. He had brought her as close to it as he possibly could. She grasped the wooden palings with both hands. Her knees felt a little wobbly. She glanced sideways, and saw distress on his face.

'I would take you out there if I could,' he whispered. 'I promise you that I would. But my uncle would be so furious.'

'It's all right,' said Mary, turning sadly back, to return to the horses.

Reginald suddenly took her arm in both hands. It was a rough, almost a crude gesture, and she looked down in surprise at his hands, there on her own sleeve. But he only tightened his grip.

'They have treated you so, so badly,' he said. The sympathy cut through her, almost making her legs give way. He was supporting her now, almost carrying her, in the strong, warm grip of his hands.

Mary looked up. The mist had parted a little, and the groom was staring over now, looking right at them. Again, she felt awkward. She gathered herself together.

'Thank you,' she said, a little distantly, straightening up and finding her feet. She stumbled a little in the drifts of leaves as they walked back, as if to demonstrate to the groom that the going was rough and that she had naturally needed Reginald's help.

She'd felt something censorious in the groom's gaze, even though his face was now expressionless.

She could tell, too, that Reginald was discomforted by the man, as he instructed him to hand over Old Humphrey's reins, and then there was the fuss of her own remounting. But for the whole of the ride back Mary smiled to herself. In Reginald's tone, she had also detected a protective note, protective of her. She didn't really care about the groom or what he thought.

Someone, at last, was taking care of her.

Chapter 18

February 1534, Hatfield

The next morning, Mary felt like riding again, but she didn't want to wear her severe and unbecoming black habit. She wanted to wear a dark red, wine-coloured gown, which the chamber women had spent the previous afternoon cutting down and restitching so that it would fit her.

Mary had a sour suspicion that it might have been a cast-off of Anne Boleyn's, left behind when she visited Hatfield. But she did not think too closely about that. She loved the richness of it, the splendour. Sadly, though, it was much too big, for she had shrunk almost to nothing during her stay in the gallery. She squeezed her arms with her fingers. Yes, good bread and good butter were already making a difference. Yes, they were less like sticks. As each day went past, she was growing stronger again, returning to life.

In the morning Reginald came, as if for his orders, as if this was now a regular thing.

'I shall walk in the garden,' said Mary, in the queenly, offhand manner that she remembered from her mother. She acted so aloof because she could not bear to reveal how very pleased to see him he was.

Instantly he was bowing, and twitching the corners of his mouth to show that he knew that he was being a little bit over the top.

'It shall be the greatest honour and privilege of my life, madam,' he said, 'to escort you, if you will accept such a base fellow?'

Mary could hardly keep her own face straight at his mockery of the obsequious rules of court life.

Her father would certainly have called him a damned puppy, and maybe, if he was in good spirits, he would have challenged Reginald to an arm wrestle. How she longed to see her father again in a fine mood. Not as he was now, all cold, and acting as if she were dead.

She damped the thought down.

'Yes, indeed, Master Reginald,' was what she managed to say, in a deliberately faraway tone.

They went down the grand stairway together, this time with Reginald walking respectfully behind her. Along the way they passed maids and off-duty nurses. Each of them sprang back to stand against the walls while Mary passed. Their eyes bored down diligently into the floor.

Mary was reminded of the groom who had yesterday made her feel uncomfortable simply by looking at her and Reginald.

I *can walk with Lady Shelton's nephew,* she told herself. *There's nothing to see here. I'm doing nothing wrong.*

Secretly, though, Mary knew in her heart that Reginald wasn't just another servant. She quickly and determinedly switched her thoughts away from the question of what God, and her mother, might think of these antics.

She was glad when they reached the lower

gallery, and stepped out through its doorway into the parterre. There were the remains of a light frost on the grass.

'There's frost, madam!' Reginald was saying. 'Shall I fetch you pattens?' She saw that the sun, by shining through it, was turning his brown hair almost auburn.

Mary did not want to stomp about the gardens with clumsy feet on elevated overshoes. That was not at all the impression that she'd wanted to create in her wine-red dress.

'No, no, it's all right, I shall keep to the path,' she said.

But he insisted on squatting down, almost to the ground, to inspect her footwear.

'Little velvet slippers!' he said, in a mock astonishment. 'They are hardly suitable for the garden.'

Mary could not help laughing a little at his prim and proper tone.

'Oh, and you have never had wet feet yourself?' she asked. 'Obviously not, for that would have led to a cold, which would have carried you off to Heaven in a trice. It's *so* dangerous to walk on wet grass.'

She spoke ironically, catching Reginald's own tone.

'I cannot deny it,' he said. 'My mother often has been driven to despair by my getting soaked in the rain, or falling off Old Humphrey into a ditch of water, and coming home all wet. But, as you say, it has not yet done me ... real harm.'

Mary bowed her head. He had emphasised the last two words – *real harm* – in a way that suggested he knew all about her imprisonment in the attics, and was glad it was over, and was sorry that it had happened.

She wanted to ask him about her relationship with his cousin, and who exactly had ordered the imprisonment, but ... no. That would cast a shadow on the day. It was such a crisp, golden morning, and the path extended ahead so invitingly, that she could bear to do nothing other than place her hand through the crook of his extended arm and begin to walk.

As they reached the end of the garden, they turned back to see the vast extent of the house rising up before them. Now Mary could see the windows of the gallery at the top, where she had been imprisoned, and the chimneys on the roof where she had found the arrows. The archer must have fired from the rough grasses of the meadow beyond the garden. She looked for the spot, although she said nothing to Reginald. The risk had been considerable, Mary thought. The archer could have been spotted from any one of the numerous windows on this side of the house. She thanked God, silently, for the loyalty of her mother's friends.

'It's a fine house, isn't it?' said Reginald, seeing that she was looking back up at the glazing of the windows as it flashed in the sun. 'How many windows can you count?'

They each started, lost their place, began again, disagreed.

Although they had stopped walking, Reginald had not given up his grasp on her arm, and as Mary pointed and laughed to show him the windows he had missed, she accidentally knocked against his side.

'Anyway,' she said eventually, as they agreed to differ on the final total, 'it looks impressive, but there are *many* more windows at my father's house of Greenwich.'

Too late, she realised that she had stepped outside the world of the sunny garden. She had hinted at things of which it was hard to speak.

Reginald at once sensed it too. He turned to her. 'I know that you must long to be at Greenwich again,' he said seriously. 'But I cannot tell you how happy I am that you are here, at Hatfield, where I may be of some service.'

'I am afraid,' she said sadly, 'that my father does not want me there any more. I'm not sure if I shall ever see Greenwich again.'

Somehow, even though Reginald's cousin was her deadly enemy, he had made her feel that she could trust him with her real thoughts.

'I am sure,' Reginald said, 'that the king is proud of his … beautiful daughter.'

Now he was looking deeply into her eyes, so much so that Mary's thoughts of the court, and of palaces, and of the hatefulness of her father, faded away. She stared back. The mysterious archer, the windows all forgotten, she felt she was almost drowning in his gaze. Grey. His eyes were grey, like her own. She could see where his beard would come, too, when he was a man.

'I thank you for your service,' she said at last, simply. 'I have been lonely these last weeks.'

'Oh! I can't imagine how lonely.'

With an impulsive movement, he snatched her hand and carried it up to his lips. Before she knew what had happened, he had kissed it.

Gentlemen had often kissed her hand before, countless gentlemen, upon being introduced as ambassadors, or as gentlemen coming into waiting, or indeed as officers of her own household like Sir John.

But no one had ever kissed her knuckles with passion, almost as if he could not help doing it and lacked the power to prevent himself.

Mary snatched back her hand, as if scalded by hot water. It was such a potent feeling, so unexpected.

'Forgive me, forgive me,' he was saying quickly, taking off his cap and twisting it in his hands. 'I was too violent; I was overcome.' She noticed, with a pang, a red stain rising up his throat. She had made him feel bad. For a second, she felt a little thrill of power.

Mary's own hands were at chest level, trying to silence the noisy beating of her heart. She stepped back.

'Nothing to forgive, Reginald,' she said, as lightly as she could. 'Now, we must not argue, or they will see us from the house. And armed men will doubtless be sent forth to rescue me.'

His eyes swivelled sideways at the great cliff of the house, with all its many serried ranks of windows. Yes, who knew what lay within? Who knew what eyes were watching?

She held out her hand. Sedately, he tucked it into the crook of his arm. At a slow, decorous pace, he led her back through the garden. Just like any gentleman in waiting, with a care for his mistress's velvet slippers.

Chapter 19

February 1534, Hatfield

The next day, Mary wondered how she could possibly fill the time until Reginald came to pay her a morning call.

She was up and out of bed at dawn, and she even voluntarily climbed the dreaded stairs to the high gallery. She wanted to walk up and down there, in order to build up her strength again. It had been awful feeling so weak. She wanted to be strong, to ride better and faster, so as to be able to keep up with Old Humphrey.

Or, in truth, she wanted to be able to keep up with Reginald.

When the sun had been up about an hour, she knew that the kitchen fires would have been got going, and that her breakfast would be on its way. She was back in her room, ready and waiting, a good long time before anything happened.

This morning, Lady Shelton brought the tray, and having set it down, hovered around the room, tidying, straightening, making sure that Mary had enough butter.

'It's all fine, thank you, Lady Shelton,' Mary said, rather wishing that she would go away. She almost preferred Lady Shelton as gaoler rather than serving woman; it was easier to keep her role straight. It was hard to hate someone who stood now by the fire, looking worried.

What had Lady Shelton to worry about? Mary wondered, a little crossly. Lady Shelton hadn't a care in the world. She had a niece on the throne, and all queens looked after their relatives. She had a fine position here at Hatfield, as governess to a baby princess. It was hardly a difficult job.

But there was no doubt about it, Lady Shelton was anxious. The high dome of her forehead was deeply lined with concern, and she seemed on the point of speaking. Mary stopped chewing. She had never seen Lady Shelton looking uncertain before.

Mary took pity on her, and decided to begin a conversation. 'I hope to ride again this morning,' she said, 'with your nephew Reginald.'

Lady Shelton gave a sharp little intake of breath, and crossed her arms.

What on earth was going on with the woman?

Mary's curiosity was pricked.

'Will you … perhaps sit down, my lady?' she asked, for Lady Shelton was clearly in distress. Lady Shelton sank, slowly, on to the very edge of the stool by the fireplace. Her fingers were twitching and making false starts of their own.

'Reginald,' she said at last, in her deep voice – surprisingly deep, as it came from such a long, narrow throat.

'Yes, your nephew …' Mary was astonished that she needed reminding.

'I would advise you to have a care with Reginald,' she said.

Mary stared, aghast. What on earth? Lady Shelton stood up abruptly, turned her back upon Mary, and hurried out of the room.

Mary was left anguished, ashamed, suspecting that she had overstepped some invisible line with Reginald. But she was not quite sure. She liked and trusted him. He was so … solid. He was someone you could rely on, and she was so tired of relying on herself.

And yet something was unsettling. First the groom, now Lady Shelton. What did they know that Mary didn't? When Reginald came that morning, she told one of the waiting women to send him away, to say that she was not well.

***

Later Mary felt so anxious, and so cooped up in her room, that she decided to walk by herself in the park. What was the mystery at which Lady Shelton had hinted? She had advised Mary to have a care, and all her returning feelings of happiness and normality had collapsed at once, like a house of cards. Mary felt that she was positively stooping beneath the weight of many cares.

Above all, Mary felt suspicious. She believed that Reginald cared about her – she, oh, she certainly cared about him. Was Lady Shelton just trying to take him away from her? To hurt her?

Perhaps walking would help. If Mary hurried across the long grass meadow at the side of the house and hid herself quickly among the trees, maybe she could pass undetected? And if anyone, Sir John, for example, tried to stop her, she would blaze at him like her mother used to do. Mary certainly felt, her thoughts in turmoil as they were, that she could blaze at anybody today.

She tried to slink out of the garden door, but of course the gardener was there, and, oh, the insolent groom too. She felt their eyes on her back, and kept it ramrod straight as she went into the meadow. Of course, the long, wet grass was soaking her skirt. But under their gaze she did not like to lift it out of the way, and pretended she didn't mind.

Among the trees, she found a little path, which led to a tiny stone turret, twins of the ones on the house's roof. It must be a pleasant, cool, stony place to sit on a hot day. On this gusty day in February, it was unpleasantly cold. But at least the turret might shield Mary from the wind.

Mary eyed the leafless trees in the woods behind her. There were one or two snowdrops beginning to poke through. What would happen if she bolted? Would she be able to get far enough away, on her own two feet, so that no one would recognise her and bring her back to Hatfield? She knew that Sir John would send men on fast horses to hunt her down. And even if she did escape, there was nowhere she wanted to go except to her mother, and she could scarcely achieve that. She didn't even know where her mother was.

Trapped. Mary was trapped. She had scarcely sat down in the little stone turret and begun to brood once more, when she heard someone moving quickly through the grass. She half stood, ready to blaze away at whichever servant it was.

But it wasn't the groom. It was the person she had hoped, but also feared, to see.

'Mary,' Reginald said, bowing formally. 'I would have come sooner if you'd let me know you were walking out.'

'I didn't ask for you,' she said coldly, paying no heed to the note of reproach in his voice.

He looked almost … hurt. 'Oh,' he said. 'Do you prefer your own company?'

'I am … not well,' she said, with a hint of a stammer.

'They told me that this morning,' he said, 'but soon after I heard you playing on the virginals. You are very, very good, you know,' he added, almost shyly. 'I thought it was the professional musician, but they told me it was you.'

So he had been listening! Perhaps he had been listening outside the door of her rooms? Despite herself, Mary's heart beat a little faster. When she had been playing, she had to admit, she had half the time been imagining that he was listening. And he really had been!

But she also felt very wary of him after what Lady Shelton had said. Who was she meant to trust?

Mary noticed that Reginald was still standing, his hat in his hand before him, head bowed. His shoulders looked very broad indeed as he towered up above her. But his lowered chin told her that he was completely hers to command.

Slowly, Mary patted the stone bench next to her. This was wrong of her, she knew, to invite a young man to be seated in her presence. But she couldn't resist.

He sat beside her, as young men do, with his legs apart, and dangled his hat awkwardly in his hands. The easy conversation of earlier days simply would not flow.

'Was it your mother who taught you how to play?' he asked, at length.

'No,' Mary said. 'I had fine teachers. I always enjoyed playing. But the instrument here is poor. I can play much better on my own one, which, oh, it must still be at Hunsdon.'

'Do you … do you hear good news of your mother's health?'

Mary bristled up like a cat.

'Why do you ask about my mother?' she asked at once, suspiciously.

'I only …' He turned his cap round and round in his hands. His cheeks were crimson again. He seemed as awkward as she did. He turned his eyes towards her, and Mary saw that they were troubled.

'Reginald,' Mary said again, slowly and seriously, 'why do you want to know? Did someone … ask you to ask me?'

Abruptly, he stood up and left her. He was striding

across the meadow towards the house. He was clasping the back of his head in both hands, as if it hurt him.

'Reginald!' she half shouted. She had not dismissed him. What did he mean by leaving her presence without permission, without a bow?

Mary stared after him, her mouth half open. She noticed that his velvet cap, with its feather, still lay next to her on the stone bench. She was convinced that he had not meant to be rude, but was in some inexplicable confusion and distress. Sighing, she picked up his cap and stroked it with her cold fingers. She imagined that it still contained the faint warmth and smell of his hair. She sniffed it, her eyes closed, and its scent did indeed bring him back immediately into her mind, almost as if he were sitting beside her once again.

What on earth was going on?

***

Mary, too, hurried back into the house, through the darkening late afternoon. Once in her rooms, she demanded that Lady Shelton be summoned immediately.

'Tell me,' Mary insisted, 'what did you mean this morning when you warned me about Reginald?'

Lady Shelton shook her head mutely, and Mary could see that there was grave concern in her eyes.

'Tell me!' she half shouted.

Yes, that felt better.

But she had also seen Lady Shelton wince. Mary suddenly remembered that when her father had shouted like that, it made people too afraid to answer him and tell him what he wanted to know. She took a deep breath and tried again.

'What are you afraid of?' Mary asked, more gently. 'Is it Sir John?'

Lady Shelton gave one of her tight little shakes of the head.

'Is it … Master Cromwell?' Mary tried again.

This did the trick. Lady Shelton stood and went over near the window, and addressed her words out through the panes. It was as if she had now made up her mind, and would tell all her thoughts. But she kept her back turned, as if she were ashamed.

'It was … a plot,' Lady Shelton said. 'I think you should know that the young man you call Reginald is *not* my nephew. He's not really a gentleman, even, although he's a good actor and knows how to pass for one. He was sent to … entrap you. It was Master Cromwell's orders. I have thought for a long time now that it is wrong to treat you, a senseless young girl, as you have been treated. But this was the last straw.'

Senseless? Mary stiffened.

But her head told her that this was no time to worry about a stray word. It was more important to gather information than it was to feel offended.

'Entrap me how? Tell me at once.'

It was rude, but Mary couldn't be bothered with the formality of using Lady Shelton's name or skirting around the matter.

She responded in kind.

'He was sent to … lead you astray,' Lady Shelton said. 'Into immorality. And I could see yesterday, in the garden, that it was starting to work.'

Now it was Mary's turn to wince. Had Lady Shelton been watching from the window? She squirmed inside as she remembered how she had laughed and smiled up into Reginald's face as they walked. Yes, she had clung too hard to his arm. Had Lady Shelton even seen him kissing her hand? Had she been that easy to read?

Mary felt a fiery blush rising into her face.

'It was all Master Cromwell's orders,' Lady Shelton said. There was no doubt that she was in great anguish herself, her narrow shoulders shaking. 'And it was shameful, shameful. I want no further part in it.' She turned, decisively, and handed Mary a piece of paper. 'Here,' she said. 'I know you will not believe me unless you read it for yourself. You are an intelligent girl. In fact, I think that you are one of the cleverest girls I have met.'

Mary slowly took the paper, but did not look at it at once. This was all so strange and implausible.

'And you, Lady Shelton, why are you telling me this?'

Lady Shelton's sharp fingers almost scratched the air.

'Because it is *wrong*,' she said fiercely. 'I am here because my niece has become queen. She has commanded me, through Master Cromwell, to execute this plot, just as she commanded my husband to lock you up in the attic. But she is getting too … too high-handed. I fear that she will fly too near the sun and come tumbling down. I cannot be glad to see her exercise her wrath upon … a defenceless girl.'

'Ah, but it was Master Cromwell who had me brought down from the attic,' Mary said, instantly spotting a flaw in Lady Shelton's speech. She leaned back in her chair. But her eyes never left Lady Shelton. Could she trust her? Was this some new trap? Where was Reginald? *Who* was Reginald?

'Read it,' Lady Shelton implored her. 'You'll see all the orders came from … from my niece the queen, through him. We were to starve you, then if that failed, to send a young man, to … seduce you. When Master Cromwell came to "rescue" you –' here Lady Shelton gave a hollow laugh – 'it was only to appear well in your eyes. So that he might persuade you to sign to the succession, and renounce your position.'

Unwillingly, Mary unfolded the paper. It was addressed to Sir John and Lady Shelton, and dated from the time of her arrival at Hatfield.

Firstly, the paper read, *cause her to die of grief or in some other way.*

That was starvation and loneliness, Mary thought. That was what they were trying to do when she was kept up in the attics. Well, that hadn't worked. Her mother's spies had seen to that, with the secret food, and even more importantly, the secret encouragement, the signs that showed she had not been forgotten.

Next, it went on, *compel her to renounce her rights, by marrying some low fellow, or falling prey to lust, so that the king may have a pretext and excuse for disinheriting her.*

Mary looked up, startled. Lady Shelton met her gaze, and sadly nodded.

'He will be gone from here by tonight,' she said. 'I have sent him away, and his ridiculous horse too. I think he has lost the stomach for his work anyway.'

Mary knew that she meant Reginald, and despite herself, her heart sank.

So, was she never to see him again?

Despite everything Lady Shelton had just said, she could scarcely believe it. Surely Reginald had meant everything he said yesterday, when he apologised, when he said that passion had caused him roughly to seize her hand?

Her knuckles came to life and gave her a tingling sensation as she remembered the moment in the garden.

But today he had been strange, more than strange, in his behaviour. Discourteous, and different.

'If this is true …'

Lady Shelton butted in, uncharacteristically rude.

'It is true, I swear it!'

'If this is true,' Mary began again. Her voice was beginning to quaver.

It was beginning to dawn on her that she had started to feel happy once again, despite everything, and now she was plunged once more into darkness. Mary couldn't help but wonder how much her father knew of this. Or if he even cared. 'If this is true, then why do you tell me so? Surely you should not? What will happen to you when the … plot fails?'

Lady Shelton turned away again, so that Mary

could not see her face. It suddenly occurred to Mary that Lady Shelton had done a very brave thing in disobeying her orders.

'I don't know,' Lady Shelton said simply. 'I don't know.'

There was no 'princess', there was no 'Your Highness', there was not even a 'my lady'. But Mary didn't mind. She felt chilled, and humiliated. She had been so nearly taken in by Reginald. Yes, she was a senseless girl. And what would Anne and Master Cromwell do next, both to Lady Shelton and to Mary herself?

Chapter 20

March 1534, Hatfield

The answer was, to Mary's surprise, that she was left alone. Life continued quietly at Hatfield. She had reached an unspoken agreement with Lady Shelton that she would give no trouble, and in return would receive none.

She stayed in her chamber, reading, or helping the serving women to sew clothes for poor people, or else she walked in the high gallery within the house. She never played her virginals, as a sort of punishment to herself for her pride. Ashamed of how she had behaved with Reginald, she wore no outfit other than her old black dress.

She thought of Reginald often. He had made her wonder what it would really be like to be in love, and to be married. When she had written her dutiful letters to *le duc* or *le emperour*, she'd never thought of either of them as a real person, someone to sit down with, for example, in order to eat dinner. She certainly could imagine eating with Reginald. Or at least, she could have done, before it all went strange and sour.

For a few days, he had stopped her from feeling lonely.

More than ever Mary wanted her mother, to ask her what it was like to be married. She remembered Catherine warning her that a princess must live much within herself, and Mary wished she had listened better at the time. It would be so nice to live with someone you could trust and rely upon. Had it ever been like that for her mother and father? Had their marriage ever been happy? Mary longed to feel part of a family. To live with people who cared for her.

Even a sister would do.

Sometimes Mary heard her own baby half-sister crying through the wall. But Mary took great care to avoid Elizabeth in person, so as to sidestep the issue of having to recognise her sister's status. Twice a day, Elizabeth's nurses took her out from her rooms for an airing. As the nursery ran to a predictable timetable, Mary could retreat to her own room at mid-morning and mid-afternoon to avoid them. It made her sad. But this was how it had to be.

The so-called Queen Anne did not come again. Her father did not come again. Yet Mary suspected that they hadn't simply forgotten about her. They were just biding their time. That Anne was devilishly good at biding her time. Mary knew that she must be hoping to give the king a boy baby as well as a girl. That would increase her power even more.

One morning a few weeks later, she heard an unusual bustle among the servants below, and knew that someone important had arrived at Hatfield. Her first fear was that it was Anne. The thought of her stepmother, and her plots, made Mary so queasy that she was even a tiny bit relieved when she saw that it was a large, moony man's face peering around the edge of her door. Master Cromwell was still in his travelling boots, she saw, and had come at once to see her.

'Straight up!' he said. 'I've come straight up to see you. How are you?' He was moving towards her across the room, and Mary did her best not to flinch.

'Well, thank you,' she said cautiously. She might easily have misread the expression on his face as concerned, friendly, eager to please her. But then, she had seen that terrible piece of paper, with Anne Boleyn's orders so clearly written out upon it, and signed with his name. She could not trust this agent of her enemy.

'May I sit?' he asked, flopping himself down in her chair. 'You're so kind. I'm sure you'll humour an old man who cannot ride as hard as he used to.'

He groaned a little, stretched a little. Yes, he did look tired.

'But it's made up for,' he went on, 'by seeing how things are here. You are blooming, my dear.' He looked at her with satisfaction, almost with pride.

Mary knew that she was looking less ghostlike than when he had last been at Hatfield and had 'freed' her from the attics. She was plumper now, perhaps a little more glossy, and her hair was growing fast and thick.

'What do you want?'

She decided that she could not bear to play his little game that they were friends. It was just too awful. She crossed her arms, cradling each elbow of her black dress. She knew that this made her look angular, and sulky. She revelled in the feeling.

He sighed.

'Oh, my dear,' he wheezed, 'don't be like that. I was hoping that you and I could be allies, you know, working together. I can do all sorts of things for you, you know. Restore you to your father's good graces. Get you out of here.'

'Get me my title back?'

Mary snapped it out.

'Ah, I'm glad that you admit that it is no longer yours,' Master Cromwell said smoothly. 'Does this mean you retract that paper you signed saying that you still stake a claim to it?'

Mary instantly regretted her mistake.

'It was a figure of speech,' she said. 'Of course I am, and have always been, a princess. It's just that no one here recognises it.'

He sighed again, moving in his chair and lifting his toes towards the fire.

'It's just a word,' he said comfortably. 'Just a little word. Isn't it more important that you have your health, and your happiness, and your family?'

'I have none of those things,' Mary said stiffly.

It suddenly pierced her, like an arrow, that she wanted her family, her mother and father, oh, so badly. Her health and her happiness were as nothing to her, besides them.

'You could be with your father and mother in a trice!' he said shrewdly, as if reading her mind. 'There's just one little signature that stands between you and them. Look, here is where it goes.'

He had his paper ready again. 'Just … acknowledge your sister as princess. That's all it takes, one signature, and you'll be welcome at court, or you can go to see your mother if you will. Your sister exists, doesn't she? She's real! She's here! You can't deny that.'

As if on cue, there was a thin wail from the nursery just a few rooms away.

'She's a bonny child,' he said, 'if all the reports

continue true. I haven't even been to see her yet. You, my dear, you are the main priority. It's you and your future that everyone is hoping and praying for.'

Mary noticed a gold ring twinkling on his finger. He was rich, and sleek, and well cared for, even though he spoke like a hoodlum. His clothes were not showy, and his person was rather like a sack crammed full of potatoes. There was something particularly unpleasant about his fat white fingers. She could see long, dark hairs growing on their backs.

She bowed her head. She did not believe that her father was praying for her, although she was sure that her mother did so, every single day.

'My mother, the queen of England,' she began deliberately, 'has commanded me to sign no papers until she can advise me herself, in person.'

'Ah, you call her the queen,' he said, sighing gustily again. 'I'm afraid that the Pope in Rome agrees with you there. Quite a fuss he has caused me.'

Mary started up. She had not heard this before. So her father's supposed remarriage had not been recognised in Rome! This was excellent news.

'Ah, my poor darling.' He had noticed her pleased reaction, and Mary grimaced in distaste at his pity.

'I'm afraid that what the Pope may think doesn't change a thing,' he continued. 'Your father is still married to Queen Anne Boleyn. We're in England, not Rome, and your father is the head of the Church of England. The succession still goes to their daughter. Now, if you sign here, I can promise you something that I haven't even mentioned yet, but it's something that will please you greatly.'

Mary waited, warily. To return to court would not please her greatly. Why would she want to go back to Greenwich with that wicked lady running the place?

'Your mother,' he said, 'is going to be moved again. She has been living in the Fens, you know.'

Mary did not know, and felt confused. Surely there were no royal palaces in the Fens? Surely they were full of marshes, and mosquitoes?

Yet again he noticed her reaction. Mary gave an internal wince. Her mother would not have foolishly revealed the thoughts inside her head like that. A daughter of Spain never shows pain.

'Ah yes,' Master Cromwell was saying. 'It is most unhealthy there. And the house where she is now can no longer be used. She will have to go to Kimbolton. It's a run-down old place, and people have died there, quite recently, of the putrid fever. You can save your mother from being sent there, you know. Just one signature, that's all it will take.'

Mary stared straight ahead of her, very hard. She did not see the room, or the tapestries, or the man sitting there by the fire. She focussed on a tiny crucifix that was pinned to the curtain of her bed.

She felt faint. He was a devil. He had found the very weakest spot, the very worst thing. In all her nastiest imaginings, she hadn't imagined this. He was threatening her with her mother's life.

He waited awhile but she did not speak.

Look at the cross, Mary told herself. *Just as long as you are looking at the cross nothing bad can happen.* She kept her hands clasped firmly together, in case they should reach of their own accord for the pen.

'I'll leave you to think it over,' he said lightly, and heaved himself up from his chair. 'There's no hurry, you know. I'll be here for a few days, and there will be, oh, many days after that for you to change your mind. Your mother's a healthy woman. There's no reason that she shouldn't survive living there. But she's Spanish, you know. Thin blood. Never could stand the damp, that woman.'

He was talking, bowing, puffing out his cheeks, smiling and apologising all at once.

Mary did not listen. She was thinking only of her mother. What on earth were they doing to her?

Chapter 21

February 1535, Hatfield

Mary is nineteen ...

In the end, Mary's decision had been easy. She simply imagined herself having to tell her mother, face-to-face, that she had signed away her right to the succession. She simply imagined the explosion that would surely follow. Of course she should not sign. However unhealthy it may be at the ancient crumbling castle of Kimbolton in the marshes, however dangerous it would be for Catherine to live there, Mary could not imagine any circumstances in which her fiery, vengeful mother would have wanted her to give in.

The next day, when Cromwell came to see her, she again refused to sign. And the next day after that as well. He left her sadly, shaking his head.

But there was no return to the attic or change to the daily routine.

'Time,' he said. 'Time is on my side. And it's not on your mother's side, sadly. I do hope that she continues to be well. There is so much talk of sickness in the marshes. I'm so very sorry for you both.'

Mary felt sick at his words. But she knew that she was right. Her mother would not want her to sign away her rights. Her mother really would rather die and become one of God's martyrs … if it came to that. Mary prayed that it would not.

Eventually Master Cromwell went away and left Hatfield, as Mary had suspected that he might, despite his pretence of leisure and ease. A busy man like Master Cromwell, trusted by her father, could not be expected to play lady's maid at a remote nursery house like this forever.

She heard from Lady Shelton that her sister had started to crawl, and to eat pap, but still she never saw her. And now she never received letters. This new prison of her mother's, this castle of Kimbolton, must be too strictly guarded for word to be got in or out through her friends. Mary still had the very last of her mother's letters that Clem had delivered, and kept it all the time under her dress and against her skin. She could not bear to destroy it, even though it included her mother's dangerous claim that she was still the queen, and Mary still the princess, and that anyone who said otherwise was a villain.

Then came the day when Mary was walking by herself in the gallery just before sunset, the winter daylight low and dropping fast, when a strange nursery-maid came bustling in, carrying something wrapped in a white shawl.

It was not the usual time for the baby's airing, but the little thing was crying heartily, busting and stretching her lungs. Perhaps the nurses had got tired of the sound and sent her up here out of earshot.

Mary instantly guessed that she was setting eyes upon her sister. The little white package seemed bigger than when Mary had seen it before, in the wicked lady's arms, and it was certainly making much more noise. Mary's eyes could not leave her sister, although she tried to keep on walking. She had always wanted a brother or a sister! And now that she had one, she wasn't allowed to love her. It was all so wrong, so ridiculous. How had it come to this?

Mary did not recognise the nursery-maid, and she, in turn, clearly did not know who Mary was, with her shorn hair and black dress. The maid walked up and down, rocking the bundle. Each time they passed each other in their laps of the long gallery, the nursery-maid nodded politely, just as if they were two members of the same household who had not yet happened to be introduced.

As she walked, Mary could not help but peer constantly out of the corner of her eye at the shawled creature in the nursemaid's grasp. That really was her half-sister. Her sister! She found it hard to summon up hatred for the tiny body who'd unwittingly stolen her title and caused all this anguish. Eventually the nursery-maid noticed Mary's interest, and stopped, and gestured for her to look at the little pink face more closely. Having had her cry, Elizabeth was lying there half asleep, and giving the occasional hiccup.

'She's a sweet wee thing,' said the girl. She

sounded like she came from far away, perhaps from the North of England, not from the court at all. Mary stood close, and saw the little crinkly eyes open by just a slit, and heard the light sucky sound of her sister's breathing.

The nursery-maid was treating Elizabeth purely as a baby, not as a princess.

Mary stood frozen. She couldn't quite find the right response. Should she hate? Or not? She knew that her mother would insist that she should detest this baby girl. And yet how could she hate something so weak and powerless? How could God really want her to do that?

Confused, Mary excused herself and turned quickly for the stairs, leaving her sister and the nursery-maid to walk in the gallery by themselves.

Chapter 22

February 1535, Hatfield

Late one evening, Lady Shelton and Mary were sitting wordlessly, one each side of the fireplace, and working with silks by the light of a cluster of candles. The great household of Hatfield was quiet for once, many of its members already gone to bed. It was just a normal evening of damp countryside darkness.

In the silence, a sharp tap at the door made them both jump, and then a voice was saying 'a letter, a letter for the Lady Mary'.

Mary got up at once, her heart jumping halfway up her throat. Perhaps the letter had come from her mother! Since Clem had gone away from Hatfield, Mary had received no correspondence at all, but she kept hoping that her mother's friends might somehow get some message through. Her mind quickly leapt ahead to wonder if Lady Shelton would tell Sir John that Mary had received a letter. She knew, by now, that there were many things Lady Shelton did not mention to her husband.

But no, this wasn't one of those heavily folded morsels that Clem used to deliver. This was a proper formal wax-sealed letter, placed into her hands by one of the mute serving maids.

Mary looked cautiously at it, examining it by the light of the fire. Perhaps it was from Master Cromwell? She guessed that if a letter had been delivered so openly to Hatfield then it must be something he had either written or sanctioned.

But the letter wasn't from Cromwell, Mary saw at once.

She did not recognise the seal, but on ripping it open, she saw that it was a cramped, pointed, female hand. A hand that Mary knew. She gasped.

Yes, it was from Nan. Nan! How on earth had Nan been given permission to write to her? A strong wave of longing came over Mary to see Nan again.

Perhaps Nan was going to be allowed to join her here at Hatfield? Mary's spirits lifted. Lady Shelton was sympathetic, but her loyalty might prove shallow. Nan, on the other hand, would willingly die for Mary. She knew that.

But the truth behind the letter became clear all too soon.

My dear Lady Mary, the letter began.

No 'princess', then. Mary noticed it at once. What, had even dear Nan deserted her?

I write to you from the Tower of London.

Mary looked up aghast. Lady Anne Hussey, in the Tower! Who had dared to do such a thing? To send Nan to a place where such terrible things happened? She stared at Lady Shelton, who looked back with surprise. No, Lady Shelton seemed to know nothing about this.

I write to you from the Tower of London, where I have been interrogated. My writing is not good, because neither are my hands. They used machines, Mary. They have commanded me to write, to say that you too will be brought here, and this will be done to you too, unless you agree to the succession. I pray you, Mary, to do what your olders and betters think. I pray that you might not end up like me and like this.

Mary was bent over, almost double. There was a physical pain in her heart.

'What is it?' Lady Shelton asked. She was on her feet, standing over Mary. She laid a thin white hand on Mary's arm, with almost as much gentleness as Nan herself might have done.

Mary simply gestured at the letter. As Lady Shelton read it through, her hand crept slowly upwards towards her mouth.

'And this lady ... was the governess of your household?'

'Yes,' Mary muttered, staring blankly at the table. 'She did nothing more than look after me and love me.'

She remembered Nan holding her hand, and stroking it, when they had ridden away from Mary's mother for that last time after saying goodbye.

She looked up, to catch Lady Shelton's gaze of concern.

'Have a care, Lady Shelton,' Mary said bleakly. 'It's dangerous to look after a princess.'

'Mary, you must not give in to these tactics.' Lady Shelton was standing up now, agitated. 'They are despicable,' she continued. 'I have been talking to my husband. He is troubled too, in his mind, by what my niece has asked us to do. But you must stay here, where it is safe. We can look after you, it's just that we must … obey the one rule of not letting you leave the estate. You know that if we do that, my husband and I, our lives would be forfeit? Here, sip this. You need strength.'

She was holding out a goblet of cordial. Mary understood that Lady Shelton was trying to be kind, and nodded. But the kindness was lost on her. She could only remember Nan laughing, dressing her, soothing her. She could bear it no longer.

There was a horrible spinning feeling in her head, and the world grew dark. She simply could not go on thinking, about Nan on a torture machine, about Nan in pain.

***

When Mary opened her eyes, she found herself in bed. It seemed as if some time, perhaps hours, had passed. She could hardly move her arms and legs;

they felt like cotton wadding. Lady Shelton was sitting by her side. When she observed that Mary was awake, Lady Shelton smiled. Mary saw all the sinews move at once in her elongated neck.

'Oh,' Lady Shelton said. 'Oh, but I am glad to see you awake.' She spoke as if it were a long time since she and Mary had been together. The room was still lit by candlelight, which confused Mary.

'Is it not morning yet?' Mary stuttered a little, for her tongue felt thick. 'Have I been asleep for hours?'

'Hours!' said Lady Shelton. 'Days, more like. You have been close to death.'

'But what happened?' Mary felt herself frightened, and a whimper was beginning to creep into her voice.

'Hush, hush,' said Lady Shelton. 'You're in no danger now. Nothing has changed. Remember, you are safe here, with us.'

Mary saw now that there was a man in the room, a bulky man, about the shape of Master Cromwell.

Lady Shelton saw her shrink away from the sight.

'That is Dr Butts,' she said quickly. 'Your father's own doctor. Dr Butts says that you will live, you know. You are out of danger, and here all is quiet and safe.'

'But what happened?'

Mary raised herself on her elbows, with a panicky need to know where she had been and what had happened. She felt her bodice. Yes, her mother's final letter was gone. Who had it? How could she do without it? She had loved to smooth it out between her fingers and imagine her mother writing it to her. She wished she had eaten it, like the rest. Then it would have been part of her.

'Dr Butts says …' Lady Shelton looked over her shoulder, and must have received a nod or a sign from him to continue. 'Dr Butts says that your brain was tired and overloaded. It could no longer take in new information. If you remember, you had a shock, a letter –' she paused, delicately – 'about your governess being sent to the Tower.'

Mary observed that she did not mention the letter's threat, that Mary herself would be sent to the Tower if she did not sign the paper of succession.

'And your brain was so tired, and so full, that it could not process any more information. No wonder! You have been under great strain these few weeks. Dr Butts says it is astonishing that your body and mind have stood up so well.'

Mary flopped back on her pillows.

At last, someone was taking her seriously. This doctor, her father's doctor – he was someone her father trusted! She had often heard his name. Perhaps, now that he had seen her, he would report how cruelly she had been treated. Perhaps her father would now realise that his wicked so-called wife had gone too far!

'So ... what is my sickness?' Mary asked quietly.

'It is sorrow and trouble, my dear, just sorrow and trouble.'

Now Dr Butts came over and stood by the bed, looking down at her, his forehead furrowed. His eyes in their deep sockets were perhaps brown, she thought, like the fur trimming his black gown.

'And how I am to be cured? I will never be well, never, while they go on persecuting me!'

Mary felt her voice begin to rise, almost to a shriek, and she began to clutch at the coverlet. She could feel distress and confusion returning. Nan's sad face! Nan in pain! She had caused this herself, by her stubbornness.

'I have ordered a cure,' Dr Butts said, 'and they have agreed. I have told them that they will lose your life, immediately, unless my advice is taken. And it has been. You are to be sent to live nearer to your mother, that you may feel the benefit of proximity to her. You are to be sent away from here.'

'That woman will never allow me to go,' sobbed Mary. She felt angry now, cheated, by his offer of something he had no real power to deliver.

'Oh, she will, she will,' said the doctor. 'Neither the queen nor Master Cromwell want your death upon their souls at this point. And I have told Master Cromwell that he will have just that, unless he authorises you to move. You need different air, and a different life. You are to be moved just as soon as you are strong enough. Now, drink this.'

He was holding out a little glass goblet, containing something sweet and yellowish.

Mary propped herself on one elbow just long enough to swallow it down. She coughed a little.

'Thank you, Doctor,' Mary began to say, but then

the medicine, whatever it was, seemed to be taking effect before she had even finished. She was being carried away again on a dark, slow-moving but powerful tide of sleep. Her brain, she thought, she must rest her brain. Or else she would go mad, and how could she serve her mother's purpose then? She needed to rest, and get well, in order to leave Hatfield House. She wanted never to come back.

Her final thought, just as she began to slip away, was troubling. *When I am ill,* Mary thought, *it worries them. When I approach too near to death, they grow concerned. I must remember this. This is useful.*

And she remembered her mother's last letter, containing the treasonable words that she was still and would always be queen, and that she looked forward to the time when she might become a martyr. There was something clean, and bold, and beautiful about it.

We cannot live in the way we want, her mother's letter had said, but we can choose the time we die.

Chapter 23

November 1535, Hunsdon

They moved her back to Hunsdon. Hunsdon! It was hardly any distance away from Hatfield, although it was at least situated in the direction of the house in the marshy Fens where Mary's mother was being held.

It was almost painful to be back at Hunsdon, for Mary had been there in happier times. She remembered her father striding into its Great Hall, having had a good day's hunting. She remembered her mother watching him indulgently out of the corner of her eye, while pretending not to, and her father noticing it and teasing her.

Now, without the court to give it colour, the house looked dingy and down-at-heel. Lady Shelton, who had come with Mary, sighed when they walked into the chamber where Mary was to sleep. Mary knew why: it was such a contrast to the splendid colours and furnishings of Hatfield, all acquired new or else freshened up for her sister.

'I'm sorry you've had to come with me,' Mary said. 'You'll get less credit from the court for looking after me here than you did for running my sister's household.'

Lady Shelton smiled. 'Can I tell you a secret, Mary?' she said.

Mary nodded.

'I don't want credit from the court,' Lady Shelton said plainly. 'Inside my mind, you're both of you just ... girls. You should be allowed to be girls. Nothing would make me happier than for you two sisters to be allowed to love each other and play together. Like my own children did, although they are all grown up now.' Mary smiled sadly. She agreed. She didn't hate her sister.

She remembered how this woman, so black and elegant and menacing in her gowns, had once been her gaoler. But Lady Shelton was now a friend, who ran risks and danger for Mary.

At least at Hunsdon Mary knew and remembered every nook and cranny and staircase, and here, at last, she was reunited with her own virginals. They were sadly out of tune, but she sat down at once to play. There were other things, too, left behind here, such as her books. She was delighted to see her possessions once again.

And at least she was no longer confronted with her sister's status every single day, and the Act of Succession was not brought up every other moment.

Mary knew that Dr Butts had saved her life, because after the starvation, and the isolation, and the trickery, the mental anguish of knowing that her old governess had been tortured for her sake had pushed Mary very near to the brink.

She knew that Queen Anne would stop at very little in their quest to get her to submit, but she had valuable new knowledge. She and Master Cromwell did not want her dead. That would scupper their plans. Submission was their ultimate goal, not her demise.

In the new house, it quickly became clear that contact with the outside world would be easier, much easier. It was simply impossible to keep people out of the churchyard, for example, which came right up to the windows of the house.

The very first night that Mary was to sleep at Hunsdon, back in her old room, she heard a late, low whistling from beneath her window. In no time at all Lady Shelton was at the window, speaking to someone. And soon the door was opening, and a man swathed in black was coming in. Sir Nicholas! Nicholas Carew! Mary's heart beat hard to see him.

'Princess,' he said, falling into a bow at her feet. Mary looked at Lady Shelton to see if she would be angry at the use of her old title, but she was looking intently out of the window. All Mary could see was her ramrod-straight spine.

'I see and hear nothing!' Lady Shelton called. 'I'm just watching to see if anyone comes.'

Mary smiled and shrugged at Sir Nicholas, reaching out a hand to help him up. *I was wrong about Lady Shelton*, she thought. *There was no need to hate her.*

Mary almost laughed to see Sir Nicholas staggering to his feet. She guessed he had been on a long ride.

'Yes,' he said. 'I have come from the marshes. And yes, I have a letter from your mother. Read it now, or later?'

'Later,' said Mary. 'Tell me, tell me at once, how is she?' Mary was eager to get information from an eyewitness.

'She's grown very pale, and thin,' he admitted. 'But there is, oh! Such fire in her eyes. All the time. It's not very ... nice at Kimbolton,' he admitted, as if unwilling to share many details. 'It's a dirty old place, and very cold. But it's as if she's determined to keep alive. To spite the Lady Anne Boleyn. I cannot bring myself to call her queen. Begging your pardon, madam,' he quickly added, with a shallow bow towards Lady Shelton.

Both he and Mary paused, and stood silent for a second, as if to allow Lady Shelton to defend her niece if she felt that she must.

Mary noticed a deep swallow passing down Lady Shelton's throat, but she said nothing.

'To spite the lady, then,' Sir Nicholas continued, more firmly, 'your mother is determined to stay alive. And she's determined to see you restored to your full honours, Mary, as a princess and as England's next queen. That, and the restoration of the Old Religion, is all she cares about.'

Mary knew it. All the strain she had been through, and all the terrors, were worth it to hear this approbation from her mother. Mary discovered that tears were slipping silently down her cheeks. She gulped loudly and wiped them away. Strangely, she did not care what Sir Nicholas might think. She trusted him.

'Enjoy your letter,' he said. 'I think you might find quite a lot in there about God. She talks of our Lord very frequently too.'

'And have you ... instructions for me?' Mary asked. 'About what I'm to do, I mean? Obviously, I'm to stand firm and refuse to sign away my succession. But has she got any more particular instructions for me? My life is slipping away here,' she admitted. 'The days are just passing, and I see no one, and I'm ... well, I'm just wasting time. I want to help, to do something.'

He grew grave, and drew nearer to her so that he could speak more softly. The night suddenly seemed very still and dark, and Mary wished for something, even the blowing of the wind, to make their voices seem less loud. Surely Master Cromwell had other spies about the house, even if Lady Shelton had turned.

Sir Nicholas tugged about inside the top of his boot and drew out another square of folded paper.

'You see this?' He showed her. 'No, don't touch!' Inside the paper was a pale powder. 'That's henbane. It will make you sleep.'

Mary looked at him, her eyes big and wide. 'But I don't need help to sleep,' she said. 'Since I was ill, I've scarcely been able to stay awake. I do little else,' she admitted.

'Not for you,' he said. 'For your ladies. Your mother wants you to escape from here, from Hunsdon, and to travel to the coast, where a ship is waiting to take you to the Empire. You know, to your cousin Charles. The EMPEROUR.'

Mary gasped. The emperor! The man to whom she had once been promised to in marriage. Of course, in his Catholic country she would be safe. There she need not fear her father. There she could worship in the Old Religion. But to flee away from England, her own country ... and her own mother?

'The queen,' he said, and Mary knew he meant Catherine, 'wants you to go. She wants you in safe hands. And then the emperor can invade England with an army, and drive out the evil usurping so-called "Queen" Anne.'

An invading army! Mary remembered how she had once used to laugh – even in this very room, long ago – at her mother's passion for armies and soldiers and fighting. Mary had thought that England would always be peaceful, as her father said it always would be. Her mother's fears had seemed outlandish and ridiculous.

But now, Sir Nicholas, with intense seriousness, was talking about Mary invading England with the help of a foreign power. It was treason.

The word had always sent a shiver down Mary's spine.

He saw her looking grave. 'Yes,' he said. 'It's a big step. But what else, Princess Mary? You cannot give in to them. And you cannot die a martyr, much as … dare I say it, much as your mother might hope to do so herself.'

Mary frowned. She hated to admit that her

mother might not live to a ripe age; become an old lady. But she had for some time suspected that her mother wished to die as a martyr. That, surely, was her plan. At the right moment, when she was ready, Catherine would give her life to make her point.

Inside Mary, a little voice wailed. *All I wanted was a mother and a father and a brother and a sister to love me*, it said. *Is that too much to ask?*

She bowed her head. It was only Sir Nicholas's matter-of-fact voice that brought her back to herself.

'Now, here are the arrangements.' He coughed. 'Lady Shelton, if you please, will you join us? You are to act quickly, before the household settles into a routine here at Hunsdon,' he explained. 'Tomorrow night, if Lady Shelton agrees, she and your other ladies will drink henbane with their wine. All of it. It won't hurt them,' he added quickly, seeing Mary's grimace, 'just cause them to sleep very deeply. Like you did at Hatfield, do you remember?'

Mary turned her head. Something ... something was nagging at her mind.

'Yes, at Hatfield,' he said. 'Do you remember how you slept?'

Oh, what a sleep it had been – deep, dreamless, for many, many days. He could see that of course she remembered. He held her eye, and nodded.

'Well,' he said softly, 'it was our friend Dr Butts who helped you to sleep then, with henbane, just like this. He drugged you, to make you look near death, so that they would change the regime and move you away from Hatfield, where you were totally inaccessible, to a house like this, where we can meet and talk. It was all part of the plan.'

'But Dr Butts wasn't even in the house when I fell ill!' Mary was astonished and dismayed. 'He came later!' Did she know nothing about what was really going on? Was all the world deceiving her? Using her as a pawn in their games?

'Oh, yes, he *was* in the house,' Sir Nicholas continued. 'He was already at Hatfield visiting the … your sister, Elizabeth. That's why he was on hand with his drugs and his medicine chest. But the henbane, which he administered, made you look near death, and there were many witnesses to that in the household. Everyone could see how sick you were.'

'But Dr Butts is my father's doctor!' Mary

exclaimed, looking from Sir Nicholas to Lady Shelton. She was looking fixedly down at the floor. Oh! So Lady Shelton had been in the know too.

'Your mother, the queen,' Sir Nicholas said, 'has many friends. Even in your father's household. There are many, many people in this country who still love her – many more than who love the so-called Queen Anne. People who want to help your mother, and so they want to help you. That's why you must carry out this plan – all these people are depending on you.'

'All right,' said Mary. She thought it over.

'I will see my cousin the emperor again at last,' she added. 'I think that last time I was only five years old.'

***

It was agreed. The very next night. The worst moment for Mary was actually leaving her room, with Lady Shelton and the other gentlewomen snoring gently, in various awkward poses, upon their chairs and benches by the fire. One of the ladies had even slipped to the floor, and lay curled up like a cat on the hearthrug. The women had all drunk the henbane with pleasure. They wanted Mary to escape, but didn't want to be blamed for letting her go.

They had been so happy to swallow the drugged drink that it had almost been like a party, with laughing and hiccuping as it began to take hold. It had been so nearly like fun that Mary felt that she hadn't done anything really bad. In fact, she'd done nothing she couldn't imagine justifying to God, if she had to, as she stood before the gates of Heaven.

But for a princess of England to go running at night into the care of a foreign power? This was bad. This was treason.

But it was also inevitable, if it were her mother's wish.

Mary noiselessly left the warm room, and the sleeping ladies, and crept down the stairs. Then she was moving along the entryway to the churchyard, one hand trailing along the cold stone of the wall to guide her in the dimness.

There was a gleam of moonlight out in the churchyard, and she had almost got as far as the field beyond, when she heard the tread of the guards on the stone flags of the path. She shrank back into the darker shade of a yew tree. She was shivering now, feeling just as vulnerable as when those arrows had come whizzing past her on the roof.

The crunching of feet came nearer, and she could hear low muttering voices. Then they were fading away again. How often did they patrol through the churchyard? she wondered. Were there other eyes watching as well? She also wondered exactly who was waiting for her in the field, waiting to escort her to the coast. She had on her warmest grey gown for travelling, but had brought with her nothing else but a present her mother had once given her: a prayer book.

Mary picked up the hem of her gown, so that it wouldn't drag on the wet grass, and started forward again. The gleam of the sundial in the moonlight made her jump; for a second she had thought it the blade of a sword. Then she was under the shade of the tall dark hedge between the churchyard and the field. She worked her way along it, again feeling lightly with her hand. Its leaves were cold and wet, and before long the fingertips of her gloves became soaked. Soon she reached the gate and stealthily peered round the edge of the hedge. She hoped that she'd be able to spy out the lie of the land, rather than show herself all at once.

In the field there were horses, yes, dark shapes moving against the sky. And was that a figure coming towards her over the grass? She could see a dark lantern; a lantern with a shade slit to produce just a little sliver of light. It must be in a man's hand, for now he was lifting it up, to cast a wider glow. Yes, he must be waiting for her. Who else could it be?

Seizing all her courage in both hands, Mary pushed open the gate and launched herself out into the field, half stumbling in the tussocks. The grass was long and deep. The man with the lantern was almost wading, waddling towards her. Was that the long grass or … was he rather a fat man, with short legs?

Mary suddenly stood stock-still. All at once she felt the intense chill of the dark air. This wasn't Sir Nicholas. It was Master Cromwell.

'Good evening, my lady,' he said.

She stood, staring at him, breathing shallow and fast. 'You are enjoying the beautiful evening, are you, my dear?'

Now there were other men coming forward, surrounding her. No one was violent; no one was rough. They came forward gently, quietly, like shepherds trying to catch a frightened sheep. But still they came. Cromwell held them all in his silky spell. 'Shall we escort you back into the house?' he asked. 'It really is very wet underfoot out here. My shoes are soaked. I hope I don't catch cold.'

He hitched his fur gown higher on his shoulders.

'Come on, help the Lady Mary!' he said over his shoulder. 'I really can't manage everything,' he muttered. 'I'm too clumsy, an old man like me. Someone take this lantern.'

Someone did, so that Master Cromwell could move unimpeded towards Mary, his hand outstretched. She did her best to ignore it, turning in the wet grass, but the footing was so insecure that she teetered. And so it was with his soft grasp upon her upper arm that she returned through the churchyard gate. Something had gone wrong. A message had miscarried. Or maybe she shouldn't have trusted Sir Nicholas.

**

An hour later, Mary was back once again in her room. She was staring, dead-eyed, at the wall, lying on her bed with her back towards the room. She was doing and feeling absolutely nothing. She'd finally given up thinking of ways to get a message to the emperor's men, waiting somewhere out there in the darkness to take her to the coast. There were no options. Without the knowledge of who had betrayed her plans, she had eventually accepted that there was no chance whatsoever of escape.

Master Cromwell was still fussing around somewhere in the room behind her, like an anxious hen. He had insisted upon her being brought hot water, and hot drinks, and more furs. To see and hear him, Mary thought, you'd think him nothing more than an overanxious nursemaid concerned about his charge's foolish night-time wander in the churchyard when she ought to have been in bed. His solicitude made her want to vomit.

When he had bustled Mary through the chamber door about an hour ago, the sound had clearly woken up her ladies. Mary saw them stirring, and stretching themselves, shifting around on their chairs and benches; beginning to ask questions about what had happened, then realising that perhaps it was better not to.

Mary was very careful to avoid the gaze of Lady

Shelton. She thought that through timidity, through not wanting to injure the ladies, she probably hadn't given them enough henbane. And yet it hadn't mattered. Someone, somewhere had revealed the plot.

But still, the henbane. Mary realised that there was one final way left to escape from this stuffy, overheated room, this gloomy, run-down house, these watchful, sleepless eyes. Take enough of the henbane and she would sleep for good ...

She began to imagine the wicked Queen Anne's anger. What would she do if Mary slipped from her grasp, almost from right between her fingers? What if she died before she ever submitted? The thought of Anne's wrath actually made Mary smile at the wall.

She plucked out the paper packet from where she had hidden it under her pillows. She lifted it up close to her eyes, and stared at it intently.

'NO!'

It was Lady Shelton, seizing the packet from between Mary's fingers and hissing out the word. Mary squinted at her. She could hear Master Cromwell talking his way out of the room, taking leave of the other ladies and maintaining his constant, jovial burble. She was glad to hear it fading away as he moved off down the stairs.

'I want only to be one of God's martyrs,' Mary said, curling herself back into an even tighter ball. 'Give it back to me.'

But Lady Shelton was shaking her by the shoulders, vigorously, almost violently.

'There are to be no deaths,' she said, almost spitting out the words. 'I could kill your mother with my own hands, for what she has done to you.'

Lady Shelton's anger shocked Mary out of her despairing, trance-like state. She was so surprised that she dropped the henbane on to the coverlet. Lady Shelton's face, she saw, had real wrath upon it.

'She may wish to die, to please herself,' Lady Shelton said, 'but your mother should wish to live, and to live for you. It is a sin to die before God commands it, Mary, a deep and terrible sin. Do not commit that sin. Never even think about it. Not even to escape evil is it worth having that sin upon your soul. Yes, the world looks dark, but remember, *the tide will turn.*'

Mary leaned back on the pillows.

She found herself shocked at Lady Shelton's words.

Lady Shelton was her friend, surely. But her friends always praised, never criticised Mary's mother. Was it even possible that God *didn't* want her to become one of his martyrs? In that case, she had had a near miss.

'Yes,' Lady Shelton said savagely, somehow reading Mary's face. 'Yes, your mother may want to die. But only because it would hurt and anger your father. They should not use you this way in their quarrels. You are *a girl*. They must let you be a girl!'

'But,' Mary whispered, 'I'm not just a girl. I'm a princess.'

Lady Shelton wasn't listening. She was over at the fireplace, burning the paper with the remains of the henbane in it.

'Never, never will I credit it,' Lady Shelton was muttering to herself, while she angrily poked at the logs to make the flames leap up. 'They may be a king and a queen, but *never* was there such a terrible pair of parents.'

The word made Mary think. She didn't miss the king and queen at all, she realised. She was sad, she had been so sad, because she missed her father and mother.

Chapter 24

January 1536, Hunsdon

L ady Shelton was right; things did get better. But first they had to get worse. It was a dark day when news came of Mary's mother's death, but it was hardly surprising. She would never forget how kindly, how gently, Lady Shelton broke it to her.

'Her last words were of the king, your father,' Lady Shelton said. 'But you know what she was thinking? She was thinking of you and your position. Everyone knows that her last words would be reported back to him. And that it would be best for you if her last words were that she was still loyal to him, despite … everything.'

Mary *did* know what Lady Shelton meant. Her

mother had explained to her, in her own words, about the importance of doing things for show, for politics. But still it gave her a stabbing pain in the stomach to think that her mother had spoken of her father in her last breath, and not of Mary herself. Still playing the game, then, to the very end.

Mary sat silent and bereft. Her mother had died as a queen, not as Mary's mother. She felt a great big mother-shaped hole in her heart.

'And there's more.'

Mary couldn't believe that there was 'more'. More what? More accusations? She sat utterly still, staring into the flaming heart of the fire.

She knew that some people would think that she had caused her own mother's death by her refusal to sign the Act of Succession. Should she have signed? Should she have had her mother released from that dangerous prison in the marshes? Had Master Cromwell been right after all?

'No,' said Lady Shelton fiercely. 'I can see what you are thinking. It was not your fault, it was never your fault. She ... it's almost as if she wanted to die.'

'But that means she wanted to leave me behind,' Mary said blankly.

'To leave you behind to continue the fight, for her rights, and for your own. And that's why you can't give up now. Do you understand what your mother's death means, for your own position?'

What a stupid question, Mary cried inside her heart. *It means I am all alone in the world!* She almost wanted to plunge her hand into the flames, so that they would eat her up and she could travel to Heaven, where her mother would be waiting for her.

But Lady Shelton was gently snapping her fingers in Mary's face, even cradling her cheek, bringing her back to reality.

'This is what I believe,' Lady Shelton was saying. 'I believe that your mother did not, perhaps ... resist death, as much as a Christian should have. But I also believe that she did it for a reason, which is to set you free, Mary.'

Mary could not bear this foolishness.

'How does this *set me free*, Lady Shelton?' she said. Indeed, she half shouted the words. 'Am I not still practically in prison?'

Lady Shelton sat down beside Mary's chair, crouching on the floor-rushes. They had long got past being gaoler and prisoner, even mistress and servant. They were a team. She clutched Mary's hand and squeezed it to get her full attention. Slowly, Mary's mind returned from Kimbolton and the marshes, and back to her bedchamber here at Hunsdon.

Lady Shelton was waiting for her to be ready. *Well,* Mary thought, *perhaps I had better listen, at least, to what she has to say.*

'Now,' Lady Shelton began. 'You understand that your father ... cast aside your mother to marry my niece Anne?' Mary nodded. She didn't like to think about it, but it was true. It had been her father's strange desire for that woman, a desire she couldn't fully comprehend, that had destroyed her family.

'It was a big thing to do,' Lady Shelton continued, 'very difficult, very expensive. And, as a result, my niece was very secure in her position as queen. If the king gave *her* up, why then, it would all have been a waste of time. Offending the Pope, offending the emperor, offending all right-thinking people.'

Mary nodded. Yes, he could be as obstinate as her mother, in his own way. Once her father had set his heart on the lady, it would have hurt his pride to have changed his mind.

'Pig,' she whispered. 'He is a pig.'

'He's a pig,' Lady Shelton agreed, 'but a pig caught in a trap. Because my niece the queen –' here she glanced round to make absolutely sure the room was entirely empty – 'has not been able to make him happy in recent months. He is tired of her. Everyone at court is saying that now your mother is dead, he will set her aside.'

'Set *her* aside?' Mary must have looked as surprised as she felt. Surely this miserable blight upon her life, her stepmother, would never lift. Surely not.

'Yes!' whispered Lady Shelton, her voice low. 'Not even I love my niece any longer,' she admitted. She was speaking very, very softly. 'She has turned proud, and cruel. It could be that she will not be queen for much longer. The people support you, Mary. The guards have told me that they have intercepted, oh, more letters and messages and gifts than

277

ever, this last week.' Lady Shelton's voice grew warm, and full of consolation. 'Your time is coming,' she continued. 'The tide will turn. Remember I told you that before?'

Mary did remember – it had been the night of her failed escape. If Master Cromwell hadn't prevented her from leaving that night, she would perhaps have had the chance to see her mother one last time to say goodbye.

'My mother also said that,' Mary admitted. 'She said that the Wheel of Fortune may take me high but also cast me low.'

'Well,' said Lady Shelton, almost tartly. 'I think you have been about as low as is possible. I think that God will decide that the tide in your fortunes must change. And what else would your mother say?'

Mary had told Lady Shelton often enough, since they had become confidantes, about what her mother was like.

'She would tell me to be a bloody stubborn blood-drinker,' she said begrudgingly. 'And to wait for better days.'

***

It was a few weeks later that Lady Shelton's prediction took solid form. Mary was still at Hunsdon, sitting at the high table in the hall, pretending to eat. She had lost the gains she had made since her release from the Hatfield attics, and could feel herself growing thin and gaunt again. With her mother dead, she hardly cared.

This particular dinner hour, there was a commotion in the courtyard. *Just like the time the Duke of Norfolk came to take me away to Hatfield*, Mary thought warily. The idea led to Nan Hussey, who back then had been sitting at the table with Mary. Mary had no idea where Nan was now. She prayed that Nan had been allowed to retire quietly to the Husseys' country estates, to recover her health after her incarceration in the Tower.

The door burst open, just as before.

This time it was two gentlemen who came in, bristling slightly, and shooting each other glances out of the corners of their eyes. Clearly they were at odds. There was an elaborate pantomime of courtesy about who should approach her first.

Mary was surprised to realise that they were

Sir Nicholas Carew and Master Cromwell, two people she had never thought to see together.

Master Cromwell stretched out his arms as he approached the table with his usual waddling gait. He pushed his fists into his arched back, stiff as usual from the ride.

'Yes, we are odd travelling fellows, are we not?'

Sir Nicholas merely glowered at him. He paced in with grace, like a cat. A few hours on horseback from London presented him with no challenge.

'Yes, we are here *together*,' Sir Nicholas said, in response to the question that Mary was looking at him with. 'We come in common cause. But first things first. I am deeply, deeply sorry for the death of your mother, the queen.'

His hat was off his head, and he dipped his chin so low that his beard touched his chest. Although his gesture almost hid his face, Mary could tell that he was sincerely moved.

She inclined her head, willing herself to remain glacially calm and not to give way to her grief. She needed her wits about her. She had an overwhelming need to question Sir Nicholas. What could he tell her? When had he last seen her mother? But she did not want to ask him anything in the presence of that cruel slug Master Cromwell.

'I too offer my deepest condolences,' said Cromwell now, reaching for one of Mary's hands as if to give it a consolatory caress. She snatched it back out of reach, but quickly turned the movement into the action of rising from her chair, as if she had meant to do so anyway. She could not bear the thought of his fat fingers touching hers. But she also felt that she could not afford to antagonise him entirely.

All three of them stood there, uncertain. Eventually, Mary's curiosity overcame her.

'So, why are you here?' she asked bluntly, sitting down again.

She knew that there must be two serving men standing just outside the door. 'Have you been offered ale?' she asked, loud enough for them to hear. The enquiring face of one of the men appeared round the door frame, ready to take an order.

'No, no,' said Master Cromwell irritably. 'We don't need refreshments. Now shut the door, my good man, and leave us alone.'

As the door banged shut, Mary thought warily that maybe she should have requested a witness for what might follow. She imagined the way that Lady Shelton would raise her eyebrows and look coolly down her nose at Cromwell's squat figure. She drew herself up to do the same thing.

'To business,' Cromwell said.

He splatted his palm down heartily on the table near to her. Sir Nicholas slowly turned his gaze upon Cromwell, as if to signal distaste, but not his entire dismissal of what Cromwell was about to say.

'It's the death of your mother, the late dowager princess,' Cromwell began, 'that changes everything. As you know, your father, the king, is growing a little tired of your stepmother, the queen.'

Mary gasped. She had heard these rumours, but to have such treasonable matters spelled out, aloud! It was unthinkable.

'I thought you were a good friend to the Lady Anne Boleyn,' she said distantly. 'Do you now betray her, as you betrayed my mother, and me?'

'I serve the king,' said Master Cromwell point-edly. 'Not the queen. I have no agenda other than to serve the needs of my royal master. He knows this, and has rewarded me well for it. My master now requires me to … rid him of a marriage that has become an encumbrance and a chore to him. He endured it as long as your mother endured, out of, well, propriety and dignity.'

'He didn't want to admit he was wrong, more like!'

Sir Nicholas had snorted the sentence with derision, but his words made Mary stiffen. It was all very well her thinking bad thoughts about her father, but it was different when other people put them into words.

Master Cromwell paused, and gave Sir Nicholas a stare, but responded no further.

'Propriety,' he started up again blandly. 'But matters are different now. He has found the queen to have become … somewhat trying. And there is the matter of an heir.'

'But the … but what about my sister, my half-sister, what about her?'

Mary had so nearly said the Princess Elizabeth, words that were constantly joined together in her presence, but she saved herself just in time.

'Well, obviously a girl's not good enough, and Queen Anne has failed to produce a boy,' Master Cromwell said. 'Your father has decided to try again, with a new queen, someone young, and fertile, and able to give the country what it needs – a baby boy. So your sister is like you now, just the plain "Lady Elizabeth".'

Mary could hardly take it in. She had been demoted from princess to mere lady; Elizabeth had taken her place. But only for a time, it seemed. Were they both unacceptable, now that their mothers had fallen from favour? Mary felt a pang of pity for the tiny baby she'd seen at Hatfield. She'd been difficult to dislike, so young and defenceless. It would become even harder to hate her, if she too was going to suffer as Mary had.

Why could their father not just love them as they were? Mary curled up her fists as the thought came into her mind. She and her sister had nothing wrong with them. Nothing! Apart from everything, it seemed, in their father's eyes. They were not boys.

Cromwell watched her absorbing the informa-tion. 'Yes,' he said, going back to what he'd said at first. 'The Queen Anne no longer has friends at court. All good people will now do the king's will in seeking to have her set aside. All friends of the old queen –' here he gave a slight bow to Sir Nicholas – 'will make common cause with us too.'

Mary saw it now. Her mother's death, just as Lady Shelton had predicted, had brought about enormous changes. Now the wicked lady was to be brought low!

But how on earth could she play a part?

'And what has this to do with me?'

She asked the question out of genuine curiosity. The two men exchanged glances without speaking. It was as if they were silently recommitting themselves to a plan previously discussed. Again, Sir Nicholas nodded.

'We need information,' Cromwell said at last. 'At Hatfield House, the queen's daughter, Elizabeth, was kept under … certain conditions. You know yourself what they were. You were her serving woman. It was by the queen's orders that you were put in that position, and deprived of your liberty, and I believe deprived of food. And indeed, towards the end of your stay, I believe that you were poisoned. Is that true? We need your word for this. Your evidence will join the list, the *growing* list, I might add, of the misdeeds of the queen.'

Mary thought of the paper, signed by both Anne and Cromwell himself, which listed the conditions under which she was to be kept. But where was that paper now? She did not know. Even if she had the paper, he would surely protect himself by saying he had drawn it up at the request of the lady.

'So you ask me to draw up an account of what happened at Hatfield, the ways in which my rights were infringed, for my father's attention, do you mean?'

'Oh no,' said Sir Nicholas, 'for the law courts. For nothing in this country proceeds without recourse to the law.'

He spoke bitterly, and Mary knew he was thinking of how her mother's rights had been twisted and mangled and set aside by the lawyers eager to do the king's will. They did his dirty work for him.

'And if I don't ... agree to say what I know?' Mary asked tentatively.

'Then it will be hard for us – for *us*, as we are allies now – to get you brought back to court, and back into your father's good grace,' said Cromwell. 'You can continue here, just as you are. Or you can return to court, and once again be a princess. He will welcome you back.'

'Oh,' cried Mary. 'But this is what my mother wanted all along!'

She imagined the smile on her father's face, his arms spread wide, as she ran into them. But would it really be like that?

'Indeed, it is what your mother wanted,' said Cromwell gently. 'But she was too stubborn to get it. Will you be cleverer than she was, and please me, and your other good friend Sir Nicholas, very greatly? Will you accept the offer?'

Mary looked at Sir Nicholas. He slowly nodded.

'I *was* drugged,' she said. 'I was given henbane. It is true. They poisoned me.'

Cromwell smiled, slow and triumphant.

'Thank you, my dear!' he said. 'Now we can get you back to court.'

Back to court. How did Mary feel about that? She

looked down at her hands, twisted in her lap, and pressed them hard together, so hard that the knuckles went white.

'I may as well go back to court,' she said. 'Now that my mother is dead, there is nothing else for me to do.'

'Good girl,' said Cromwell again, encouragingly, as if she were a dog or a small child. His condescension did nothing to reduce Mary's feeling that she had been played. She was still his puppet in this endless game.

Chapter 25

And despite Master Cromwell's promise, she was left waiting. And waiting. Mary felt utterly stuck at Hunsdon House, waiting for a summons from court that never came.

Spring slipped into early summer. The news came through of the wicked lady's fall and her death under the executioner's blade at the Tower of London. It was just as Cromwell had foretold. Mary shivered when she thought of his power, his network of allies, his almost magical ability to get things done. Yet now, she reassured herself, he was on her side. They were working together.

Mary could hardly credit the tales that she was told of Queen Anne's trial, the accusations made against her in the law court that she had been unfaithful to the king. Mary wondered if the truth had been tweaked there too, just as it had in the testimony about poison that she'd given to Master Cromwell to use.

It was perfectly true that she had been poisoned, but it was by her mother's friends, rather than the wicked lady. And now the lady was dead! Killed at the orders of her own father.

That's a person I met, many times, Mary told herself, *who lives no longer. I talked to her, sat with her. I hated her, truly hated her. But did I really want her dead? Did God want her to die?*

She did not really know.

Mary remembered herself as a young princess at Greenwich Palace, who'd complained that she was never allowed to play with other girls or read her books. Instead she was always supposed to be engaged upon a fight to the death. The old Mary seemed like a different person. *My mother knew, somehow,* Mary told herself, *what was going to happen. It was a fight to the death between that lady and me, and I won.*

At that moment, Mary knew exactly what God wanted her to feel, just as if He had spoken the words in her ear. She shivered with the sheer thrill of being still alive.

She wanted to run crazy through the orchard, and gallop on a horse as fast as Old Humphrey, and jump higher in a dance than any other courtier could. She was ready to live life again, at court.

She thought long and hard about how she would confront her father, challenge him with having abandoned her. She wanted to make him feel bad for having let her suffer for so long. She'd heard that he hadn't even visited her mother's grave. He sent no letter to acknowledge that Mary herself might be devastated. She wanted to make him pay for all that, before she could let him love her again.

But the summons from court still did not come.

Mary wanted to write to Master Cromwell, asking what was happening, but she feared to do so. It was all too dangerous to commit to paper. She had entered into a deal with the Devil. She'd agreed that if she gave testimony against Queen Anne, he would bring her back to court and to her father. It was …

troubling, to say the least. She did not want to admit in a letter that she'd had any part in Anne's downfall.

Mary slipped almost back into her old life at Hunsdon, walking, reading books, mooning about, waiting with Lady Shelton for something to happen.

But in those days her mother had been alive, pulling the strings behind the scenes, and there had always been the hope of a letter.

'Ironic, isn't it,' Mary said to Lady Shelton, 'that I am actually eager to hear from Master Cromwell, who has done me so many wrongs?'

'But can't you just live quietly, here at Hunsdon, and be satisfied?' Lady Shelton asked Mary. There was an unfamiliar note of exasperation in her voice. Mary looked at her, really looked at her, for the first time in some weeks. Lady Shelton was a little paler, her eyebrows less black. There was a thread or three of iron grey, now, in her hair. *She's growing older*, Mary thought.

'Do you really want to go back to court?' Lady Shelton continued. 'It's a snake pit where … where my niece and your stepmother has just lost her life!'

Mary knew the answer. She had been taught it at her mother's knee.

'Yes, I do,' she said. 'I have to fight in the great fight. Princesses can't just slip away or disappear. I have grown soft, living here. Some people, enemies of my mother, will always think that I'm a threat. I have to fight and win, or die. Really and truly. It is my duty.'

Lady Shelton sighed, and gave half a smile. 'There's no denying it,' she said amicably, as she unfolded her rangy body from the seat in preparation for leaving the room, 'you're your mother's daughter.'

Despite this, there was no opportunity for combat for many weeks. It was June before anything happened.

Finally, one warm day, Sir Nicholas Carew arrived, looking haggard and tired. There was a new stoop in his back. Mary remembered her mother's frequent murmur, as they sat together in the stands at the tournament, that Sir Nicholas was 'such a handsome man'. No longer was this quite true.

Mary thought this as he came striding over the grass towards her where she sat in the orchard. Her book was on her lap, although in fact she had just been sitting, staring vacantly, and thinking.

'Cromwell has betrayed you,' Sir Nicholas said shortly, as soon as their greetings were over. 'He used your evidence in the secret trial. I heard as much from a man who was there. But he hasn't got the king to agree to your return, as he should have done.'

'But why not?' cried Mary, incensed, taking in only part of what Sir Nicholas had said, the fact that she could not go back to court. 'But he promised!'

Her heart had been set on leaving this dreary place, on starting a new life. Probably her mother would not have approved of her deal with Cromwell. Now she felt, like a kick in the teeth, that her mother would have been right.

'He is a devil,' Sir Nicholas said, 'but a powerful one. And now I have something else to say that I think will displease you.'

Mary shook her head impatiently. She couldn't

take any more bad news. But then she remembered that he was trying to help.

'The sticking point,' he said delicately, 'is the Act of Succession. It has become an … obstacle, in your father's mind, that must be overcome before you return to your former place, despite the help you gave in bringing about the fall of the lady. And Master Cromwell has guaranteed to get your agreement to it.'

'You mean, he *still* wants me to sign to say that I am not a princess?'

Now Sir Nicholas bowed his head, eyes trained on the grass.

'Yes,' he said. 'Your father still denies that his marriage to your mother was valid. I thought he might change his mind after Queen Anne's death, but he is stubborn, stubborn on this one thing. He thinks people will judge him.'

'Judge him?' Mary cried. 'But he is the king. He cannot be judged like ordinary men. He can do anything he wants!'

'Oh, but your mother would be sad to hear you saying that,' he said gruffly, turning away. 'He should obey the laws of God.'

'How dare *you* tell me what my mother would or wouldn't want?' Mary snapped.

'Let us not quarrel, princess,' he said soothingly. 'I spoke in haste. And you remind me of her, oh, so much, especially when you stand there with your hands clenched like that.'

Mary realised what she was doing, and gave a rueful smile. Yes, she was standing in the very stance of a blood-drinker. She tried to relax.

'Your mother,' Sir Nicholas went on, 'was very … rigid in her views. It cost her greatly. It cost her something she valued above everything else, which was your company.'

Mary knew it.

'But what would you have me do?' she asked. 'I don't understand. If I can't go back to court, will I just stay here forever? Moulding away? Until someone remembers and decides that it really would be easier all round if I were to die, and perhaps moves me to the marshes myself. It's intolerable!'

'I think,' Sir Nicholas said gently, then stopped. Mary felt a terrible foreboding chill as she suddenly guessed what was to come.

'I think it's time to compromise,' he said. 'If you sign, you can return to court, and build up the position of your friends. If the king were to die tomorrow then you, probably, would be acclaimed queen. He still has no son. But you must be on the spot, and known to powerful people. You can also speak up, at court, for our Old Religion, which Anne Boleyn did her best to destroy. And now her cursed soul has gone down to Hell, you can be with your father again. And perhaps be happy.'

'But I don't trust Master Cromwell!' Mary cried. 'And you spoke of my mother! She would not approve. You know I can never do this!'

'Ah, but …' He shuffled the papers in his hand. Mary saw that there were several. 'Your mother's friends have been in secret communication with your mother's nephew overseas, the emperor. He has obtained this for you.'

Mary took it from him, examining it carefully. 'It's an absolution from the Pope,' he explained. 'You sign that you agree to the Act of Succession, and to your new status, then the very next minute you sign the absolution. This means that God will forgive you, and all good Catholics will know that you have not betrayed your innermost self. It is just for show.'

Mary sighed. So it had come to this. Even her supporters, the only people who seemed on her side, were advising her to give in – with a get-out clause.

'I will think about it,' she said. 'Leave them here with me.'

'Tonight, princess,' he said. 'I advise you to sign tonight. You should return to court and start to rebuild a life there. You should give heart to your mother's friends, and you should see your father again. After all, you are his heir.'

He turned and went into the house. Mary sat on in the orchard, her mind lost in a maze of pros and cons. She felt unable to move, even to get warm. After a while she noticed that she was thirsty, but it was as if someone else were feeling the sensation, not her.

It grew cold as the sun began to set and dew started to gather on the grass.

She picked up both papers again. She suspected,

somehow, that in the last few minutes she had made up her mind what to do, but she didn't want to admit it just yet.

When she lifted her head, she could see the guards in the field beyond the orchard, and Sir Nicholas waiting patiently by the garden gate. Against the lighted windows of the house she could see Lady Shelton's shape, watching and waiting. Everyone was watching and waiting and wanting her to sign.

Slowly, resignedly, Mary went inside. Her feet felt immensely heavy. She could hold out against her enemies, but not against her friends. At eleven o'clock, with a leaden heart, she picked up the pen and put her name to each of the two papers.

'I'm sorry, Mother,' she whispered, very softly, as her pen moved.

But then she heard, as if from far away, her mother's own voice.

'Press harder, Mary. The letters are too faint.'

For an instant Mary felt something like a little worm stirring inside her. She scarcely recognised it. It took her a minute or two to realise that it was something she hadn't felt for a long time. It was hope.

If she couldn't have them both, then it would be better to live with at least one of her parents once again. She couldn't bear to be alone any longer.

PART THREE

RETURN TO COURT

Chapter 26

July 1536, Hackney

Mary waited uneasily for several days, wondering exactly how and when she would be allowed to return to court. In her mind, she often turned over her decision to sign her succession rights away – and sometimes she regretted it. But more often she felt that she'd done the right thing. She would once again be the king's daughter. And now that her sister was demoted, maybe one day she might become queen.

Mary began to fret about her clothes and possessions. Having been away from court for so long, she did not know what the latest styles were. And she dreaded the smiles hidden behind a hand, or the nudges glimpsed from the corner of an eye.

These things happened when the experienced courtiers judged a turnout unbecoming, or old-fashioned.

'I must be seen to be believed,' she muttered. 'But how can I make myself look like my father's daughter, stuck away out here in the countryside?'

The morning after she'd signed the act, she had asked for her best gowns to be brought to her from the royal wardrobe in London. When the wagon trundled into the courtyard at Hunsdon a few days later, Mary's serving women unpacked it, only for them to discover that hardly any of the clothes still fitted.

Of course! She had grown taller in her years of imprisonment, and plumper too. These were the gowns of a girl. Mary looked at them sadly, and tried to remember the little girl who had worn them, and what it felt like to be her. It was all so different now.

Twenty years old already, Mary thought. *When I first wore this dress, I thought that when I was twenty I'd be married, and living in France, and doing all the things the wives of kings do, like giving to charity and having children. And look at me. I'm only just beginning, all over again.*

The women got to work on alterations and expansions, but Mary guessed that the colour and the shape of the gowns wasn't quite right any more. She sighed. It would be hard work of a different kind going back to court, acting the proper part there. It was a little like going on to a battlefield, and Mary knew that she didn't have the right armour.

Well, I must go through with it now, Mary thought, turning once more to the dresses and trying to decide which one was the most becoming. *There's no turning back.*

In the event, it turned out that her return to court didn't seem to require a splendid outfit after all.

One night, Mary stayed up late with the sewing women, standing still and straight like a statue while they hung, pinned and altered her sleeves. It was weary work, slightly taxing as she could not relax, yet rather boring. As soon as she got into bed, Mary fell asleep heavily, almost as if she had been given the henbane again.

She was woken up by an insistent tapping at the door.

Strange. Because it was summer, there was a glimmer of dawn light at the window. But even with the harvesting to be done the household servants at Hunsdon were never abroad quite this early.

It was Lady Shelton. 'My dear,' she said. 'The summons has come. The king's guards are here, to take you to him.'

Mary gasped. Her feet were on the floor at once. This was what the whole household had been waiting for.

It seemed like an eternity since she had last seen her father. Now the moment had come, Mary was excited, but she was dreading it too. She'd missed him, but she also wanted to tell him how cruel he had been. Would he still love her back if she did? Surely he must still have some love in his heart for his eldest daughter?

In truth, she just didn't know.

Her heart was beating fast and loud as she reached for her dressing things.

'Congratulations,' Lady Shelton was saying, 'congratulations are due.'

Mary noticed, a little too late, that Lady Shelton

had spoken drably, without pleasure. She realised that Lady Shelton would be sad to lose her company at Hunsdon. But she had to go.

'Lady Shelton,' Mary said. 'You have been a true friend to me. Thank you.'

Lady Shelton was looking steadily at the floor, and after a moment Mary realised that she was doing so because she was too proud to show that there were tears in her eyes.

'I have been honoured to be your governess,' Lady Shelton said at last, quietly. 'My dearest wish is that your father may see you for what you are. A princess to be proud of.'

She had meant to be kind, and Mary thanked her. But her words had in fact left Mary feeling, if possible, even more tense. *Would* her father be proud of her? Lady Shelton had raised the possibility that he might not.

Soon Mary was dressed, in the plainest of her refurbished outfits. She thought that an unexpected journey so early in the day would not require the gold embroidery or cloth of silver. For a second, the former Queen Anne Boleyn came into Mary's mind.

What had she worn, for her journey to the scaffold? Had she cared what she looked like that morning? Mary quickly tried to blank out the thought. She was going to be welcomed by her father, she hoped, not slaughtered by him.

Out in the courtyard, though, Mary was brought up short by the sight of the litter that had been sent for her. It was sumptuously cushioned, and would be expertly drawn by the waiting team of fine white horses. For a moment, the memory of her winter departure from Hunsdon, riding pillion and wearing a man's smelly cloak, came to mind. Nothing could make it clearer that Mary's status was restored to her. No longer was she her sister's servant, but was once again her father's daughter.

The palanquin jolted her across fields and meadows, and the sun grew pink, and then gold. Mary tried to stop her mind from racing, racing ahead to what might happen. *Look at the fields*, she told herself, *and the trees, and all the things in the world you can't normally enjoy.*

She had plenty of opportunity to enjoy them now. She had assumed they were heading towards

Westminster or Whitehall. But as the dawn turned into day and the hours passed, Mary discovered that they weren't going to one of the royal palaces of London after all. They weren't taking the main road into town.

'To Hackney, madam,' said the mounted guard to whom she called for information. 'We're going to Hackney, to a private house there.'

Mary was left in consternation. A private house in Hackney? But surely this fine escort meant that she was going to see her father. That's what she'd been told. What could be going on? Mary was thirsty, and growing tired. Despite her nerves, she was glad when the village of Hackney came into sight.

'Not long now, my lady,' said the friendly horseman.

Mary swallowed hard. She must get used to it, and not react angrily when people used that title. She had signed to say that she accepted it. Although she'd wanted the journey to end, the knowledge that it was about to plunged her insides back into a nervous churn.

After passing through farms and fields and a

scattering of cottages, the cavalcade drew up near a timber house. It was low, small, but gentlemanlike. Mary guessed that perhaps her father had chosen it as an anonymous rendezvous. It had a neat garden, and Mary could see her father's yeoman guards, come to keep him safe, standing here and there with their battleaxes. They looked highly incongruous among the flower beds.

Now Mary was walking through the garden gate, and serving men were directing her round the back of the house. Her heart was thudding now, beating so loud that she was afraid that the usher walking so respectfully in front of her could hear it.

There, in the garden behind the house, under a bower with ivy entwined all around it, two figures were waiting. Yes! That was her father, strangely padded in appearance. Why was he wearing such a thick doublet on a July day? Mary wondered. It wasn't surprising he was looking rather red in the face.

He came towards her, yes, right out on to the grass, rather than waiting for her to come to him. Part of Mary's mind processed the compliment, in court terms, and another part noticed that there were tears standing in his eyes. The eyes themselves were a more watery blue than she remembered, and lightly rimmed in pink. But she could see no more because in a second he was giving her a great big bear hug.

In all her imaginings, Mary had not thought it would be like this. Her mother had wanted her to hate this man, to defy him. To her dismay, Mary now discovered that she could not hate him after all.

But remember Hatfield! said a little voice in her head. *Remember how he saw you and turned away?*

Mary knew she could never forget. Yet now he was looking at her with his blue eyes – after all, these were those same old blue eyes – and putting his hands on her shoulders. And now he was smiling, and pulling her roughly towards him again. Hot tears came into her own eyes. She had thought, at this moment, that she would act all proud and cool. But she could not. This was her father. He was clearly happy to see her.

'There, there,' he was saying. 'We have been parted too long, Mary. Evil people have kept us apart. I have had so many trials. How you are grown!'

She looked up at him again. He was the same …

but different. His hair, what was visible of it beneath his cap, had streaks of silver in it. And he was larger, softer. That wasn't a padded doublet; it was his belly. Mary remembered how he used to laugh and say he was growing the belly of a woman. He certainly had one now.

He, for his part, was looking at her in wonder and amazement. 'My daughter!' he was saying. 'All grown up! Why did you not come before? Why did you stay away for five whole years?'

Mary looked at him in puzzlement. Surely he knew what had been going on? Surely he knew that she had been kept prisoner?

'I feared …' she began uncertainly. 'I feared I had displeased you.'

'Well, I have been much displeased,' he said, with a wry smile. 'Your mother displeased me, and then, and then, so did another lady about whom I have little to say. But you, Mary! I always thought we were such good friends.'

Mary realised, with a sinking feeling, that he couldn't understand why she had refused to sign away her rights for so long.

She opened her mouth to explain.

Then she closed it.

Of course, it was coming back to her. This was what he was like. He'd always had a habit of forgetting the past, rewriting it. Her mother used to point out his inconsistencies. But Mary remembered, just in time to stop herself from speaking, that he had come to hate her mother for always knowing and understanding everything.

It's like a game, she thought. *I have forgotten some of the rules, these five years I haven't been playing it, but I must get back into the swing.*

'Well, I am back now,' she said, at last. 'I think wicked people have been causing trouble between us. I wish only to please and to serve you.' She did her best to curtsey, but he took her arm and prevented her.

'Not now,' he said. 'This is a private family visit. I did not want us to meet under the noses of the court.'

She realised that he was truly touched and moved to see her again. At this, her heart leapt with something strangely like pity. He had missed her too! Yet she couldn't help wondering if he were a powerful king, the man whom everyone feared, why could he not have simply called for her to come to him. Why had he allowed her to be kept prisoner until her spirit was broken? Was he not as powerful as he seemed?

'It's a family visit,' he said again, 'and I wish to introduce you to your new stepmother.'

Mary looked up, confused. Her father had beckoned, and now a lady was coming forward from the bower. She was young, very young, and fair in her colouring. She did not look at all like Mary's idea of a stepmother. Mary sensed her nervousness.

'Come on, Jane,' her father was saying, 'come along. Don't be bashful. Now, I want you two to be friends. My two beautiful girls.'

Mary looked at the lady, with her blue eyes and her pale skin. She was absolutely nothing like Mary's mother had been, stately with her golden hair, nor dark and chic like Lady Anne either.

Jane gave a shy smile and held out a hand. She spoke as if she had prepared and memorised the words. 'I am pleased to meet you, my Lady Mary,' she said. 'I am happy that we will live together all three of us in harmony.'

Mary could hardly countenance it.

The girl – she was a girl, not a woman – was hardly any older than Mary herself was. What had her father been *thinking*? If he had ended his marriage to Anne Boleyn, then surely it was only right to pause a little longer at least? Why had no one told Mary that her father had married … *again*?

It was wrong, all wrong. Mary couldn't think of anything at all gracious to say to this strange lady. She stood there tongue-tied.

'Are you … married to her?' she said abruptly, turning back to her father. He was nodding, pleased, proud. 'But what about my mother?' Mary said, her voice rising out of control. She could not help it. 'She is scarcely cold! I thought we would go together to see her grave!'

Looking at her father standing there with an enormous smile on his face, as if he was very happy to be married, it was as if he had suddenly flipped back to being a complete stranger. There was no sadness on his face at all for the death of Mary's mother. He seemed as unknown to her as this ethereal girl who had apparently become Mary's stepmother.

Mary stepped backwards and raised her arms, as if to protect herself. How else would he trick and surprise her?

The spell was broken by a voice, horribly familiar, from behind them.

'Joy!' it said. 'A joyful occasion, a family reunion.'

Mary's heart sank still further to realise that yes, it was Master Cromwell. He was coming out of the house. His arms were outstretched; there was a fat smile on his florid face. She saw her father and the new ... queen, Mary supposed that this woman must be the new queen, turn towards him eagerly.

Mary felt rebuffed, excluded. She realised that she had inched backwards, towards the bower, and that her hands had clasped themselves firmly behind her, so that there was no chance of Master Cromwell greeting or touching her. Her face had set itself into a grim mask. It was all that she could do not to cry.

'You are a blessing to us,' her father was saying.

'You have brought us back together. Never will I forget, Master Cromwell, how good you have been to this family.'

They all turned now, to look at Mary. What on earth could she say?

'Yes,' she said eventually. She swallowed hard. It was clear that something more was expected of her, but she could hardly spit out the words.

'Yes,' she said, through gritted teeth, 'I am grateful to Master Cromwell, for bringing me back into your family, sire.' The words stuck in her throat. So this was what it would be like to be back at court. Difficult.

Chapter 27

Late summer 1536, Greenwich

Within what seemed like no time at all after the first meeting at Hackney, Mary was back inside her old life as an almost-princess. At least as the daughter of the king. But it was different. Before, she hadn't taken it seriously. Now, she was deadly earnest. If surviving at court was indeed a game, it still seemed more serious than anything else.

Each day was a performance, once again, of hair, and dress, and deportment.

Now Mary cursed herself for not having taken more pleasure in the long days spent reading at Hunsdon, wearing whatever was to hand, and not having to be ... on show. She missed that sense of relaxation. But she also knew that coming back to court, being a good princess, even if she wasn't one in name, was the only way to survive.

Back at Greenwich, she found surprisingly few changes, apart from the fact that she couldn't go into the queen's rooms at will, as she had done when they were her mother's. Of course not. They were now the new Queen Jane's.

Sometimes the place seemed exactly like before, but sometimes the changes seemed to Mary almost dizzying. Since she had been here last, as princess to Queen Catherine, there had been not one but two different queens living in this palace, sitting at the high table, leading the ladies into chapel for Mass, having everyone's eyes follow them at banquets and entertainments.

Mary's mother had died in January, Anne Boleyn had died in May, and now it was only the summer! She could hardly understand how all the ladies-in-waiting and menservants and grooms lived with these astonishing turns of Fortune's wheel. But then, maybe the only way to get through it was to accept the changes blindly, like animals might, and to keep on doggedly placing one foot in front of the other.

In the last five years Mary had been imprisoned, and starved, and terribly, terribly lonely. She thought that the life of the servants she saw bustling past on their unknowable business was, in some ways, enviable. No one was likely to play cruel mind games with them.

Mary also now realised, with a pang, as she saw familiar faces among the servants at Greenwich, that many of them didn't care. A few smiled in welcome when they first saw her, or said they were glad to see her again, but the rest simply went on performing their duties, stolidly, as if she had never been away.

It seemed little had changed with her father too, although he now spent his mornings in his chamber instead of going out riding. He'd hurt his leg, Mary was told, falling heavily in a joust. She watched him at dinner, exchanging what seemed to be the same jokes with the same rowdy friends she remembered her mother disliking so much. He ate joylessly, as if it were a duty. But then he caught her looking at him, and at once raised his glass as if to toast his Mighty Princess. She could not help but smile back.

Mary was once again the second lady of the court, just as she had been before. But the new queen, Jane, was so young and so unimpressive that it was galling to have to walk behind her into the chapel, or out into the tournament yard.

Mary grew to hate the sight of the back of Jane's demure little head, especially as she wore the pointed hoods that Mary's own mother had favoured. Mary should have been happy to see a queen dressed in her mother's conservative fashion, but it also seemed strangely impertinent, as if Jane were aping someone better than herself. Anne Boleyn, Mary recalled, had never worn a hood like Catherine's, and Mary remembered being told that she thought them unflattering. But no one at Greenwich ever now mentioned her. It was as if Anne had never existed.

As she walked in the chapel procession one day Mary realised that she was lonely, perhaps even more lonely than she had been at Hunsdon, because there at least she'd had Lady Shelton, and she'd expected to be much alone.

Here at court, living back with her father, and with so many other people all around her, she had not.

The most frustrating thing of all was that she rarely saw her father without other people. Mary had never once seen him by himself, a prerequisite for talking to him about her mother, which she would have liked to do.

Was he weak, like her mother had said, or had he just made mistakes? Surely, Mary prayed, surely her father could not be utterly, knowingly malicious.

But she scarcely had the chance to find out. Mary tried once to go to her father, just to pay her respects, and maybe to chat, but she found Master Cromwell in the outer room, rubbing his hands together, and smiling to see her.

'I came to see the king,' she said shortly, in explanation of her presence.

'Oh, dear lady,' he cried, with his false-sounding sympathy, 'how unfortunate. He is busy with the queen.'

And she'd had to turn around, shoulders set, jaw grim, and march out again.

One day Sir Nicholas's creased face appeared around the corner of the door of the chamber where Mary lodged. She smiled to see him. He was among the few people with whom she could speak of her mother.

Mary nodded at her ladies, who took the hint, rose, bowed, and left.

He came forward, crinkling his eyes in his friendly way. 'Your Royal Highness,' he said quietly, sweeping a bow before taking her hand. Mary felt warm inside at the words.

She invited him to sit with her, and tell her the news.

'It's a little sensitive,' he admitted, 'but it is … um, known at court that you and the queen are not the best of friends.'

Mary almost spluttered with rage. '*Friends!*' she scoffed. 'She is not my *friend*, whatever Master Cromwell and my father might think. She is *nothing* to me. She has taken my mother's place.'

Sir Nicholas bowed his head.

'Of course, she shouldn't be sitting on the queen's throne,' he admitted.

'Yes,' said Mary stoutly, 'nor living in the queen's chambers, nor visiting my father in his when I want to visit him myself, or just … being around.'

He paused awhile, as if to allow her feelings to disperse.

'You're right,' he said.

'But?'

Mary had a feeling that something else was coming.

'But,' he said, 'I think you may misjudge her.'

'How?' cried Mary. 'There's nothing to her! She's just a good little girl!'

Possibly against his wishes, half a smile slid over Sir Nicholas's face.

'It's certainly true that she is … remarkably docile in character,' he said. 'I believe that your father, the king, finds it restful after the drama he has had, in recent years, in his private life.'

Mary nodded. With some reluctance, she conceded that her mother's behaviour, even her own behaviour, had been quite the opposite of restful.

'You should know, Princess Mary,' he went on, reaching forward and even patting her hand, 'that there is more to Queen Jane than meets the eye. She is *one of us.*'

Mary stared at him. She knew what he meant, but she could not have been more astonished. Surely Jane, the queen, followed her father's official new religion, which was now the religion of the country?

'Yes,' he said, chuckling at her surprise. 'It's surprising, isn't it? But you should know that Jane is not cut in the shape of that wicked lady. She is peace-loving, which means that she follows the old ways and worships the old God. She supports the monks and the nuns whose homes your father destroyed. You have much in common.'

Mary felt a tiny bit ashamed. Had she been too busy hating the idea of a stepmother to see who her stepmother really was?

'But what does my father think?'

Sir Nicholas coughed.

'I'm not sure,' he said delicately, 'that your father even knows.'

Mary's jaw dropped open. Her father! How little he seemed to know about anything!

Her mother's words suddenly came to mind, almost ringing in her ears.

'Soft, soft as the curds of cheese,' she'd said. 'Ready to do whatever his boon companions demand.'

Could Jane really be keeping a secret from him? After all, he'd only been married to her for a couple of months. Mary's father could not possibly know Jane that well. Mary's father was … well, it was possible to deceive him. Mary admitted that. But to deceive the king was to play with flame. For the first time, it dawned on her that maybe it was difficult to be a new wife, and a new queen.

Sir Nicholas rose.

'I would just ask you,' he said, 'on behalf of all the followers of the Old Religion, on behalf of all of the friends of the former Queen Catherine, to keep the queen's secret. It could … hurt her, if it came out.'

Mary nodded, speechless. Yes, if her father knew, it could hurt Jane indeed. And when her father was angry, she knew how far he could go.

Chapter 28

Autumn 1536, Westminster

After that, Mary looked at Jane with new eyes. It was a relief, actually, to have someone else to think about other than her father and herself. Mary wondered what Jane was really feeling. She wasn't quite sure if Jane was her rival for the position of first lady of the court, or potentially her ally.

They moved to Westminster after the news of rebellious uprisings in the North of England. If there was trouble in the land, Greenwich was too far out of town to be safe. The riots and mutinies had been in support of the nuns and the monks, whose houses were being destroyed by the king's reforms. *My mother would have been pleased*, Mary thought. *She* hated the thought of those good old women being forced out of their homes.

There was scarcely any chance to find out the answers to Mary's questions about Jane, though, and her possible support of the Old Religion, because they were never alone. Always Jane's ladies were present, or the whole court was observing them, or else Mary's father was there, acting as if everything were exactly as he wanted it. The time Mary most often found herself near to Jane was when they were seated at the table with the king, being closely observed as always by a great mass of servants and courtiers as they ate their dinner.

One day in the autumn, they were all three at the long table before the roaring fire. As usual, there were ranks of men lined up to each side of the room, with bowls and jugs and napkins, a silent audience watching the meal. *They watch us*, Mary thought, *like I might watch songbirds in a cage*. The consciousness of it made her sit up a little straighter.

She was feeling uneasy, for there were new rumours abroad of rebellion in the north, more men taking up arms against her father and Master

Cromwell's programme of closing the monasteries. But she was also hungry, and wished the servants would hurry up as they reverently placed each dish upon the table.

'Plovers,' intoned one of the gentlemen servitors. 'Rabbit pie. Venison patties. Orange wine. Dried figs.'

Mary's stomach was beginning to rumble.

'And what have you been doing today, Mary?'

She realised, while she had been staring at the food, that her father had for once asked her a direct question. So often he treated her as just part of the furniture. Mary started, trying to think of a suitable answer. There were too many people to hear, too many ears, to answer spontaneously.

But Jane spoke up.

'My stepdaughter,' she said pleasantly, 'has been practising the lute. She has taken up a new instrument, did you know, Your Majesty? Not content with the virginals alone, she's adding to her repertoire.'

It was completely true. Mary *had* been practising with her new lute, recently acquired. It seemed now that she could ask for anything she wanted, and that it would be sent up to her at once. When the lute had arrived so quickly, Mary had half wished that she could order up a friend, or a sister, in exactly the same way.

But she didn't quite understand how her step-mother could have got to know this. Perhaps Jane had sent a servant to ask, which would have been a courteous gesture. Mary bowed her head and tried to accept the compliment with grace.

'You must play for me one day, Mary,' her father said. 'I haven't played my own lute for a long time.' He wasn't really interested, she could tell, but he'd been mollified. Her lapse of attention had been overlooked. He was beaming at Jane, pleased with his wife. Jane, in turn, was smiling down at her plate, showing her dimples.

Mary thought that Jane was not truly pretty, because of her rather prominent white forehead. But when she looked happy, smiling shyly like she was at this moment, she had a peaceful face. Jane was restful for the eyes.

Mary began to feel that the atmosphere at the table was unusually warm. Very often her father was distracted at dinner, carrying on conversations about government or military matters with his gentlemen, sometimes shouting his questions to them across the room. Mary's ears lapped up any political discussion – it was interesting, but it left her and Jane little chance to speak up for themselves.

Of course they did not speak when the gentlemen were talking. Mary wondered if she might ever have her father's full attention. She had even started to worry that one day he would announce, just like that, that he had chosen a husband for her.

But today he seemed to be in a good mood.

'Father,' Mary said, taking advantage of the opportunity. 'People around the court are talking of events in the north. They're saying that rebels have been fighting against our men, and causing trouble.'

'That's right, Mary,' her father said, peeling his eyes away from Jane at last. 'But there's no need to be frightened. Not here in the town. I have plenty of fine soldiers to protect you ladies.'

'I know, Father,' Mary said. 'I'm not worried about that. But what are they rebelling *for*? Why are they unhappy?'

She had a good idea what their cause was, but she wanted to hear what he'd say. Her mother, Mary remembered, would often control a conversation without seeming to do so.

Mary's father clicked his fingers to be served some rabbit pie. He did not answer until his plate was filled, and he was eating.

'They are *rebels*, Mary,' he finally said, between mouthfuls. 'It doesn't matter what they are fighting for. The fact is that they are fighting. Disputing my authority. And yours, too, if it comes to that. As you are my daughter.'

Gallantly, he raised his glass to her, and took a long sup of wine.

Mary bobbed her head in return, to thank him for the compliment. But she couldn't go back to eating her food. She felt that he hadn't really answered the question at all.

To her surprise, Jane was leaning forward, even laying a hand upon her father's arm.

'Sire,' she was saying, low and urgent. 'They are men of principle. They fight for what they believe in. They value the monasteries, you know, and the work they do. Their hospitals, gifts to paupers and so forth. The rebels are men of God.'

Mary noticed her father freeze. His spoon hovered in mid-air. His knife fell from his other hand with a small clatter. He was utterly stiff and tense.

The silent servants, as one, seemed to give a collective cringe.

As the silence extended, Jane's hand shrank back from his arm, back into her lap. She seemed to collapse in upon herself.

'Jane,' he said at last, coldly. 'Do not concern yourself in matters that are none of your business. Politics do not concern women.'

'I only …'

Mary was amazed that Jane had the courage to go on speaking. Mary's mouth dropped open, and her eyes scanned quickly from one to the other. Surely they would not argue, not in public like this?

The king laid his finger to his lips.

'Peace, Jane,' he said, with steely menace. 'Remember what happened to my last wife.'

Mary saw Jane's face freeze, as if she'd become a

model made of wax. She saw that Jane was trying but failing to prevent her fingers from shaking as she picked up her knife, to pretend to go on eating. Mary likewise could not face another mouthful of food. She did her best to push her gravy around her plate as if she were mopping it all up.

They sat in a silence broken only by her father's noisy chewing.

When Mary dared to steal a glance at Jane, she saw that her cheek was glinting wet, as if a tear had silently slipped down the side of her nose.

At the end of the meal, Mary's father rose.

'Ladies,' he said shortly, before turning and marching out. Mary, as usual, put down her napkin and rose to follow in his wake. As she passed the queen's chair, though, she put out her hand, as quick as a flash, and lightly placed it for a second upon Jane's shoulder.

So what Sir Nicholas had said was true. Jane did follow the Old Religion too.

Chapter 29

December 1536, Fleet Street

To Mary's surprise, she'd gained someone with whom to share the ordeal of being … if not a princess, then at least one of the first ladies at court. Very often now, she went along to the queen's bedchamber so that they could get ready together.

But they hardly shared secrets, because for every minute they were still accompanied by Jane's numerous ladies. Jane didn't seem to have the confidence – the confidence which Mary's mother had possessed in abundance – to send them away.

In general, Mary found her curious stepmother to be almost dismayingly eager to please. Mary could not understand quite how Jane got through court life with her nervous, anxious manner, worried all the time about what people would think of her. But Mary could see that her father liked the fuss that she made of him.

When they were all three together, he made a great play of it, claiming that they were a family, and classing them together as his girls.

This made Mary slightly want to roll her eyes. If she were queen like Jane, she wouldn't want to be called a girl. But Jane just simpered, and lapped it up.

He thinks she's perfect, Mary said to herself. *And my father likes the idea of me, too, more than the reality. He likes telling people that I'm his daughter, and don't I look like him, and how clever I am. But he never really asks me any questions.* That was how her father preferred it, Mary realised sadly. She wondered when, if ever, he would take her seriously.

Then it was winter, nearly Christmas, and they were to ride in a splendid procession from Westminster through the city of London back towards Greenwich, the palace where they would stay for the twelve days of the festival.

Mary understood that her mother's friends, like Sir Nicholas, were very glad that she was to take part in the procession. The ride through the city with Queen Jane would be a sign of her return to … something like her former status.

Jane and Mary dressed in furs and velvet for the chilly ride, and then found themselves in the palanquin together, being lifted to a swaying shoulder level. Mary noticed the queen gulping, and holding on tight.

'It's all right,' Mary said. 'They're hardly going to drop the queen of England on the ground, are they? They'll do everything in their power to keep us up!'

'That's not what worries me,' her stepmother admitted. 'Sometimes I worry so much about doing the wrong thing that part of my mind almost forces me to do it anyway, just to spite myself.'

Mary laughed. Although the queen was supposed to be older and more powerful than herself, she sometimes felt that she had the advantage over Jane. After all, Mary had arrived at court long before Jane. After all, Mary had been born here.

The high, swaying palanquin excited Mary as much as it dismayed Jane. There was so much to be seen from up here, as they looked high over the heads of their bearers. Once the procession had started to move out of the palace courtyard, and to travel down the street, Mary noticed something unusual. The crowds lining the roadway were roaring now with excitement to see the two royal ladies. And on this occasion, she suddenly realised, the ladies-in-waiting were all travelling in a wagon, which had fallen a little distance behind.

For once, Mary noticed, they could talk without being overheard.

'We are in our own little world!' Mary observed. 'Like a ship at sea.' She'd never been on a ship, but she imagined it was thrilling, like this, to be carried upon the waves. She was looking away from Jane, to smile to the crowd, and occasionally to wave. Jane was doing the same on the other side, but she could hear Mary perfectly well.

'Yes,' Jane replied, but taking Mary more seriously than she had intended. 'We are often in a little world of our own at court,' she continued. Mary could tell from her voice that Jane, too, had spotted the rare opportunity they had to speak privately. 'You know, Mary,' she continued, 'I fear that the news of what's happening in the world is kept from us.'

Mary whipped her head round to give Jane a glance. The serene curve of her cheek looked just as usual, but in her words Mary detected something amiss. *Smile and wave, smile and wave*, Mary thought.

Across the river, the sun was shining brightly and winter-low. Jane now raised a hand to shield her eyes, and turned her head as if to avoid the rays. She was looking straight at Mary.

Suddenly she was speaking very fast and very low.

'While there is nobody to overhear us, Mary,' she said, 'I need to tell you that there is serious news from the north. My family have let me know … discreetly. The rising in the north, in Lincoln and other places, is worse than you think. In fact, there is bad news which closely concerns you. You remember Sir John Hussey?'

Mary felt a pang of regret for her forgetfulness of him.

'Oh!' she said, matching Jane's mutter, although her feeling was painfully sharp. 'It has been too long since I have seen him. And his wife, Nan, who was once my closest servant. She has … I'm afraid she has suffered in my service.'

There was a pause. Jane turned back briefly to the riverbank crowds, making great arcing waves with her arm to acknowledge their ragged cheers and cap-waving.

Mary noticed that their bearers were now moving away from the river. Great mansions and palaces were standing between the water and their road. They were getting into the City of London. There was an arch in golden tracery erected over the way, with a red and white rose in each of its spandrels. It had been knocked up overnight by carpenters, obviously, but was no less impressive and beautiful for that.

The two of them fixed smiles on their faces and craned their heads upwards. Jane clasped her hands together. 'Beautiful!' she called. The nearest members of the crowd broke into spontaneous applause.

Mary feasted her eyes on the ingenious construction for as long as she could, but then they were off again, lurching forward with a bump. 'There must be many more of these to see along the way,' she said, 'or else they would have let us spend more time, perhaps get down to thank the builders.'

But Jane was again turning towards her, and Mary saw that her pale blue eyes were elsewhere, thinking about something far removed from Christmas decorations.

'It pains me to tell you this,' she said urgently, before breaking off.

'I'm so sorry to tell you, Mary,' she began again, 'that Sir John Hussey is dead. He was on the side of the rebels, you know. Who rose up in favour of the Old Religion.' She paused, and swallowed hard. 'The religion of your mother.'

Mary clutched a hand to her side. She felt a dull ache there, like the rumble of thunder warning of a storm of feeling to come. Nan tortured … and now Sir John killed? How had this happened? This was terrible news.

But she also knew that this was no place or time to show weakness.

'Why did my father not speak of this?'

'He is very sparing with, um, with information,' Jane admitted. 'Have you not noticed that? If something displeases him, he acts as if it isn't really true. I believe he thought that when you were in … captivity. I believe he truly didn't think that anything was wrong. Master Cromwell kept telling him that you were well, and would soon submit.'

Mary stared at her.

'Wave, Mary, remember to wave,' said Jane, turning away. They were now near St Paul's and yes, here was another display – a choir of friars, dressed in golden cloaks. The sun sparkled on the jewelled crucifixes they raised as the ladies passed.

Mary looked at those crosses. What kind of a God would allow Sir John Hussey to die? A stern God, Mary thought to herself. She knew that it wasn't her place to question His will, but this was hard to bear.

Jane could sense that Mary was in pain.

'I tell you this now, Mary,' she hissed, 'because I think you have the right to know. But I beg you, tell no one else. Please act at Christmas as if nothing is amiss.'

Mary did not need to ask why.

'Don't worry,' she said, in a ragged whisper. 'I won't tell.'

They rode on further, passing narrow streets

clogged with dung, and women who looked cold, and babies who looked dirty. They were still cheering, cheering, to see the queen, and the king's eldest daughter, the Lady Mary.

'I'm not really worried about myself,' Jane said. 'I know that sooner or later I must die. But I want you to live, Mary. You are so straight, and strong, like an arrow fired from a bow. I think you will be all right.'

Mary made a quick gesture. 'But God will surely spare you until you grow very old! Why talk of dying?'

Jane was shushing Mary. Yes, unassertive Jane wanted to speak so badly that she was actually demanding Mary's attention. Mary thought she had better listen.

'Oh no, my way is set,' Jane said grimly, 'as it is for the wife of any king. I must bear a son, that's all that matters for me. As soon as I've done that no one will care what happens to me. But you know this, don't you, Mary? You have been locked up for being born royal.'

'Why did you marry him, then?' Mary could feel her eyes growing round like saucers. What a surprise it was to hear this neat little doll saying such dark, dreadful things!

Mary saw that Jane's hands were shaking slightly.

'Because I fear the king,' she said, 'and I fear Master Cromwell.'

'Master Cromwell! What has he to do with it?' Mary was aghast. She had no wish to hear more of his power and influence.

'He controls everyone, everything,' Jane said, through pale lips. 'He controls your father. It's like witchcraft. They accused the old Queen Anne of witchcraft, but it's Master Cromwell who is the wizard. Whatever he wants, he gets, and he wanted the king married to me. He thought I would be easy to manage. Well, I am easy to manage. I give very little trouble. And I will be happy to give the king a son, if I can.'

Mary took all this in, scarcely hearing the buzz of the people on the streets.

'Now smile, Mary,' the queen enjoined her. 'Remember, you have to be seen to be believed.'

The unwitting echo of her mother caused Mary's heart to skip a beat. And yes, it was exactly as her mother had warned. It may have been difficult and dangerous when she was exiled, but life could be even more difficult and dangerous here at court.

Chapter 30

January 1537, Greenwich

Christmas at Greenwich passed without any more discussion of the rebellion in the north. Mary knew that dangerous dissension was probably being whispered in corners of the palace, and that Master Cromwell would punish anyone he caught at it. Heeding Jane's warning, she made sure no one could ever accuse her personally of treason.

She felt that she had underestimated the queen. Jane, quiet Jane, was a courtier too.

At the last great Christmas feast of Twelfth Night, she and her stepmother were seated together at the High Table. Little did her father suspect, Mary thought, what a good understanding had grown up between them.

Jane now gave a tiny nod at Mary, to indicate that the king had called for another great goblet of wine. Even now, one of the servitors was placing it on the table. Jane's glance said that he'd had enough – more than enough – wine already. Taking her cue, Mary stood up from her seat.

She curtseyed to her father, then gestured to the hall to be quiet.

'Sir,' she said boldly. 'May I take the crown of the Lord of Misrule upon my own head for a moment? And turn the world upside down by asking my father to dance with me?'

Whoops arose from the assembled courtiers, and some of them burst out clapping. Mary was gratified to see surprise replaced by a slow smile on her father's face. He stood, swaying only the very tiniest bit, and gave her a low bow. Hand in hand, their wrists lifted high in the air, he led her down from the platform and into the body of the room.

The court grew solemn and quiet for the stately dance that by rights was the first of the evening. The musicians had been taken aback a little by Mary's initiative, and there was a pause of a few seconds while their leader told them which tune to play.

As they stood and waited, the eyes of the court upon them, Mary's father brought her hand to his lips to give it a smacking kiss. She saw that he was glowing with satisfaction.

'My daughter!' he said loudly, to the crowd. 'A fine lady, is she not?'

There were murmurs of approval and admiration.

Mary bowed her head and tried to hide her pleasure. But he had not finished.

'What a pity,' he said, in a lower voice, so that only those nearest to them could hear, 'that she was not a son. But my wife will soon put that right!' At that he turned to the dais, and blew a kiss towards Jane.

Then the music started up. Mary wasn't expecting it, and missed the beat for the first step of the dance. She cursed herself for losing concentration at such an important moment. Her mother would never have made such a mistake.

It was the sting of rejection, Mary realised, which had made her trip.

Why would he never, ever accept her? Why would he never be truly proud of her? It was such a simple thing, but it was all she wanted.

At the end of the dance, her father was breathless and red-faced, and Mary escorted him, rather than he her, back to the top table. She held hard to her composure, telling herself it was no time to feel upset about what he had said.

Mary called out loudly for fruit cordial 'to refresh His Majesty', and she saw, with satisfaction, that Jane had caused the goblet of wine mysteriously to disappear.

Jane herself was beaming, and reaching for his hand. As the king took it he did not release Mary's, so that all three were linked in a human chain. 'My family,' he said. Mary saw that there was even what looked like the glint of a maudlin tear in his eye. 'My beautiful girls,' he said. 'Happy together.'

Never, Mary thought, had he got it so wrong. She was not, could not be happy. She would never be good enough for him. If only she had been a boy.

Chapter 31

October 1537, Hampton Court

Mary is twenty-one …

Soon after Christmas, the king's wish that his wife Jane should give him a prince seemed likely to come to pass. It was announced that a baby boy was on its way. Mary was pleased for Jane, whom she knew to have been terribly anxious to have a baby just as soon as she could.

But Mary made certain mental reservations. How did her father know that it was a boy? That's what everyone had said last time, and her sister, Elizabeth, had been the result. Either way, Mary had signed that paper agreeing that the new baby would inherit the throne ahead of her. That still stuck in her throat.

She kept her head down and got on with life.

That actually meant keeping her head up, smiling at state occasions, dining in front of all the court, dancing with ambassadors. Nothing had been said for a long time of any marriage for Mary. She knew that she had been tainted, in the eyes of foreign princes, by her spell out of favour.

So spring turned into summer, and eventually the day drew near when Jane's baby would be born. Jane had gone away to Hampton Court Palace to give birth. Mary was at Greenwich when the order came that she was to travel to Hampton Court for the christening.

Her first question was to ask how Jane herself was, but no one could tell her. The bells ringing in the churches of the towns as she travelled through London and out the other side reassured Mary. The news was good, all good. It was indeed a boy – Mary had mixed feelings about that – but she was relieved for Jane.

At Hampton Court, she went at once to the queen's bedchamber. The door was heavily guarded, as always, but she was nodded through. At the inner door, one of the queen's ladies lifted the flap of tapestry to let Mary enter. The air was warm. Mary's nose told her that incense had been burned, but she thought she also detected a slightly horrible smell beneath it.

Mary paused to whisper fiercely, 'Is she well? Tell me the truth.'

'She *is* well, my lady,' the midwife said, bobbing her curtsey. 'Your ladyship will find her very pale. She's always been pale and now she is paler still. White like snow. But we have been bleeding her, and health is returning. How goes the prince?'

Mary realised that the woman thought she had come from the baby prince's apartments, but she hadn't even been there yet. 'He's well,' she said, somewhat distantly, moving forward into the room. It was an error not to have gone there first. Hopefully her father wouldn't hear about her lack of respect to her new baby brother, and future king.

Jane was in bed, sitting up, her hair neatly brushed over her shoulders. She looked wan indeed, but smiled when she saw Mary.

She looks like a little girl, Mary thought.

'Well done,' Mary said, and they both laughed.

'It's such a relief,' Jane admitted. 'It lasted three nights, did they tell you? It's awful, Mary, awful.'

Mary had not realised that it had taken quite so long. 'I did hear …' she said tentatively. 'One of the stable boys at Greenwich, I heard him saying to his fellow that your life was in danger. That they were thinking of cutting the child out.'

'Perhaps they were,' Jane said. 'That would have killed me.'

'No, my father wouldn't have allowed the doctors to do that,' Mary said, with decision. 'He really loves you.'

'Yes, he does love me,' she said sadly, 'but he loves his son more. I'm sure that if he could have saved the boy at my expense, he would have done. But that's all right, Mary. I was meant to be a mother, and now I am.'

She really did look exhausted, even in the glowing, warming light of the fire, but Mary could see how happy she was.

'Are they looking after you properly?' Mary asked suspiciously. She wasn't sure about the noxious scent in the air of the room.

'Oh yes,' said Jane vaguely, 'I have no complaints. Your father has been here, but he has gone away. The baby is to be the star of the christening tonight, you know.'

'I know he is,' said Mary. 'I am to walk in the procession, but he is to take the place of honour.'

'My boy and my girl,' said Jane sleepily. 'Will you be a good sister to my son, Mary? You know that I love you both.'

'I will indeed,' Mary said, 'of course I will.'

**

A couple of hours later, Mary was dressed in stiff golden tissue with heavy fur-lined sleeves. There was a red satin lining to her gown, and the stitching on her fresh new linen was finer than she had ever seen. Yes, there was no doubt that she had taken her place once more among the royal family. To the outward glance at least.

Moving stiffly in her grand and unfamiliar clothes, Mary was conducted into the lineup and shown where she should stand. Behind her, in the position of honour right at the very back of the procession, she could hear the little yelps and mews of her baby brother. He was wrapped up in an enormous golden robe of his own, and all his household staff were fussing over him. Mary looked forward to the time when perhaps he would be brought to his mother's chambers, and she and Jane could play with him a little. She also looked round for her sister, Elizabeth, who was also to be carried in the procession. Yes, there she was, too, in the arms of a courtier.

These are my brother and sister, she thought to herself, in wonder. *I have a family. A funny family, it's true, but I have a stepmother I think I could love, and a brother and a sister. I'm not just Mary all alone any more.*

For a second she dared to think of the future. Christmases together? Hunts together, feasts with Jane presiding, a tableful of people who belonged to her. For so long it had been just her mother and her, and then after that for even longer it had been Mary just on her own.

Strange and horrible things had happened, but Mary seemed to have ended up with something that she'd always wanted. It was just her father who seemed to be missing.

She heard the squeals and gurgles of her brother behind her, and smiled.

It was a dark day, scarcely light at all, and as they came out of the chapel, after the long and enchanting ceremony, the torches born in the procession were lit. A new life was in the world. The joy that Mary herself had felt seemed to have run wild through the whole court. They had drunk a cup of wine, and eaten biscuits in the chapel, and now they were returning through the galleries, cloisters, courtyards and corridors to bring the baby prince back to his mother.

Mary looked forward to seeing Jane again. There had been something not quite right, something not entirely present, about her when they had spoken. Was this the price you paid to have a son?

Chapter 32

October 1537, Hampton Court

But that evening, and the next day, Mary was refused access to the queen's bedchamber. It was the same the day after that as well.

'What's going on?' she asked the midwife suspiciously. Mary had gone over to the queen's chamber door herself to find out more. Whenever she had sent a servant with a message to ask when it would be convenient for her to visit, she had got an evasive reply.

It was the same woman to whom Mary had spoken before.

'She is well, but tired,' the woman admitted. 'We are treating her with the very best of care. We are bleeding her.'

Mary was suspicious.

'If she is well, may I not see her? She is, after all, my stepmother.'

'His Majesty's orders,' the woman mumbled, looking down at her hands.

'But His Majesty my father is not here!' Mary cried impatiently. 'How can he know what the queen's health will or will not bear? She is my step-mother, I tell you, a close relative. I know that she will want to see me. It will make her feel better.'

The woman looked up, and Mary saw that she had not really been listening to what Mary had been saying. There was something in her eyes. Was it fear?

'*What is going on?*'

Mary hissed the words fiercely, not wanting the guards in the corridor to hear, but convinced that something was up.

In answer, the woman silently stood aside, thrusting out the fold of tapestry sealing the door to let Mary pass beyond, into the area of confinement. Inside, the dim firelight made it hard to see.

Jane was lying in bed, although she had been

sitting up when Mary had seen her before the christening. She looked worse, not better. Paler. Even more like a rag doll bleached in the sun.

Mary swore under her breath. She knew what had happened. The queen's personal staff were terrified that they would be accused of not treating her correctly, so they had tried to keep her sickness a secret. Even while it grew more grave.

Mary strode quickly forward. She picked up one of Jane's limp hands and cradled it between her own.

'Mary.'

It was more of a sigh than a voice, but Jane certainly knew who she was, and Mary believed she gave a sliver of a smile in welcome. Despite her cold, greenish pallor, beads of sweat were forming on Jane's forehead.

'Mary.' Jane's parched lips were moving again, and Mary leaned close in to hear. 'Look after Edward,' the queen was saying. 'Look after Edward, do you hear?'

'What do you mean?' Mary asked in wonder. 'The whole court is looking after Edward. You have nothing to fear, Jane, and when you are well you can look after him yourself.'

Jane smiled and turned her head to one side.

'Oh no,' she said. 'There is no cure.'

'What are you saying, Jane?' Mary asked in consternation. 'Are you saying that you are really ill?'

'Yes, I am,' whispered Jane. 'I should have spoken sooner, I see that now. I haven't long.' Her head lolled to one side, as if she could no longer support it.

Jane's movement brought forward one of the nurses, with a sponge. She dipped it in water, and dabbed Jane's dry mouth, bustling forward so Mary was forced back. Other nurses were coming now, getting ready to do something to Jane. Was she to be bled again? She saw that one of them had a small blade in her hand, and another a terracotta bowl.

Mary stood, frozen in thought, while the movement stirred around her.

All of a sudden, she noted a frantic increase in the pace and tension of the medical staff.

'Call the doctor!' one of the women was saying. 'What, bring a man into the queen's chamber?' asked another. 'Yes, indeed,' came the answer, 'bring him in at once. Or it will be too late.'

Mary's hand crept up slowly to her mouth. It dawned on her that Jane was going to die, and leave her. Just as she had got her family back. This was impossible! Everything was impossible!

She barged her way forward, through the panicking women, and tried to take Jane's hand again. It felt cold, and almost lifeless. But Jane knew that she was there.

She was whispering. Mary put her head down, almost touching Jane's lips, and even so she could hardly hear.

'Mary,' Jane was saying, 'you must take care of your brother and sister. And I know it's hard to make your father listen, but you must let him know who you are. Let him know, very clearly … who you are. Speak up to him.'

Mary thought it was odd advice from the quiet, peace-loving Jane, but she decided to think about that later, when there was more time.

'I will,' said Mary. 'But don't worry. And thank you. You are …'

Mary choked. She had meant to say like a mother. But it seemed wrong. She couldn't betray her mother like that. Or could she? 'You are almost like a mother to me, Jane.'

'I *do* want to live,' Jane said, crying now, sobbing with all the strength she could muster. 'I *do* want to live to see you happy, Mary.'

Then the nurses were taking Mary aside. She realised, too late, that they wanted to shield her from the sight of the very moment that her stepmother died.

Chapter 33

October 1537, Hampton Court

Mary did not attend the ceremony which saw the queen's heart carried to its burial place in the chapel; women did not do such things. But she watched from the window as the procession set out through the gloomy courtyard. Its way was lit by the smallest pin-pricks of light from horn lanterns. It was like a shadow version of the same procession that had celebrated the christening of Jane's baby with brightly burning torches.

Mary was in Edward's nursery, rocking his cradle for herself. She had dismissed the rocking women, but of course they were hovering about only just beyond the door. They were too nervous to leave their precious charge unattended.

Every servant at court was in terror after the death of the queen. The king had raged and blamed everyone except his pale, perfect wife.

As Mary sat, and watched, and rocked, she thought over the events which had brought Jane, so sweet and pure, into danger. This business of the bearing of a son.

'Why were you not content with me, Father?' she cried silently into the blackness of the autumn sky. 'All this could have been avoided. Jane could have been saved.'

She thought again of her mother, dying in lonely bafflement in that remote castle, and Jane, dying in the midst of such splendour and courtly concern at Hampton Court.

Both of them cold and dead, in the end. What had they in common? They had tried to please the king. They had loved Mary, but had left her.

She would remember her promise to Jane, to look after this baby boy, even if he had taken her place as heir. And then there was her sister, Elizabeth, likewise ousted from the succession. Mary could not be a good princess, it seemed. She could not, it seemed, be a good daughter, not good enough for her father, at any rate. But she would at least be a good sister. At the very least she would try.

There was a heavy step in the passage outside, and Mary looked up angrily. She had told the rockers and nurses that she would treat Edward carefully, and that he would come to no harm. Why could they not leave her alone?

To her surprise, it wasn't the nurse, or the groom of Edward's chambers.

It was her father. His face was a smeary mess of tears, and his cheeks were full and red. Mary stood up uncertainly.

'I have been with Jane,' he said, with a great snuffle.

Mary looked at him, almost ashamed. She was not supposed to see him like this; no one was. When he said he had been with Jane, she realised, he meant he had been sitting in her rooms beside her corpse. The queen's body was laid out on her bed, surrounded by lit tapers, waiting for its ceremonial transportation to the royal vault at Windsor.

He came over to the cradle and leaned in to look at Edward. Putting out his great hand ever so carefully, he gave his son the gentlest of strokes on his cheek. Mary had not thought that her father could have been so deft.

Then he straightened, and sniffed again, and rubbed his eyes with the heels of his hands. Blinking them open, he looked at her closely.

'Mary,' he said, 'I need to talk to you.'

Mary's stomach did an uncomfortable flip. What now? What wickedness or devilry had he in mind? Was the Wheel of Fortune about to hurl her even lower?

'No, no,' he said, seeing her expression.

With a cracking report from his knees, he settled his bulk down on to a stool near hers, so that they were on the same level. Mary glanced around. It was so unusual to be all alone with her father. In fact, she could never remember it having happened before.

But wait, he was speaking and she wasn't even listening.

'... before she died,' he was saying, 'Jane told me something of what happened to you. She was so angry. Lord love me! I had never seen her speak so passionately as she did then. I didn't know she had it in her.

Now listen, I promise you, Mary, I did not know what they did to you. I promise you that I never ordered it to happen. I wanted you to sign the Act of Succession, of course I did, but they exceeded my orders.'

'But, Father,' Mary responded, 'it *was* difficult. But I … have survived. You can see that. I'm here, and I'm well, and I'm very, very sad about Jane, but really and truly I have survived.'

She bowed her head. She'd spoken almost without thought. In the end, when she'd had the chance to tell him how she hated what he'd done, it turned out that it didn't matter. It was in the past. She had come through it. What mattered was the future – Edward's, Elizabeth's and hers.

There was a long pause. Was this what he wanted to hear? How would he react?

Finally he looked up at her.

'You *have* survived,' he said. 'More than that, you have thrived. And I want to speak to you of years to come.'

He continued, louder, pulling at Mary's hand and bringing her to her feet. He was speaking now as if there were other people in the room with them.

'Mary is to be the first lady of the court,' he declaimed, 'and to bring up her sister and her brother. My three children will all live together and love each other. She needs to continue the work that Jane started.'

Mary gasped.

For almost as long as she could remember, every time her father had opened his mouth she'd wished his words had been a little different. But now he was saying exactly what she would have willed.

'You, Mary,' he continued, 'have been a true child to me. And you were a true daughter to … to the sweetest lady who ever walked the earth, and before her, to a Spanish princess who did her best to please me for many years.'

He was hardly apologising. But he was suggesting that sometimes, in the past, he had been wrong.

A warm, calm feeling came over Mary.

'I do see that you have survived my mistakes,' he said, addressing her directly now, simply and straightforwardly.

They stood there, face-to-face. It struck Mary that he was speaking to her as if she were grown up, as if they were equals.

'I think that you have the fire and spirit of your mother,' he continued, 'but I think you also have the grace and patience of Jane. If the worst should happen –' and here he looked at Edward in his crib – 'I think you would make a good queen.'

Then he turned away and tucked his thumbs into the armholes of his gown as if to rest his arms. It made him look weary, like an old man.

'Probably a better queen than I am king,' he muttered. 'I'm getting old, and tired, and people take advantage of me.' He paused. 'And who knows, Mary? I have three children, but God is cruel. Many men lose their sons before they are grown. And then, why then, Mary will be queen.'

He raised his hand, and laid it heavily upon her shoulder. Mary covered it with her own hand, and dipped her chin to her chest.

She took several deep breaths.

'Father,' she said eventually, 'I think I have been waiting for you to say that for my whole life.'

Epilogue

Why I Wrote This Book

This is a story based on events from real-life history. Some characters and happenings have been missed out, but it's absolutely true that the Princess Mary was demoted to 'Lady Mary' when Anne Boleyn's daughter, Elizabeth, was born. Mary really did refuse to eat rather than accept the situation. And she did finally give in, return to court, and attend her baby brother Edward's christening.

What happened next after the story told in *Lady Mary* finishes? King Henry the Eighth wasn't wrong to worry that something bad might one day befall Mary's brother, Edward.

Edward spent a good deal of time with Mary

during his childhood, but then, at the age of fifteen, he suddenly fell ill, and died.

By that time, the supporters of Anne Boleyn's New Religion – they'd end up being called Protestants – had once again grown strong at court. They argued that the next ruler should be neither Mary, nor Elizabeth, but their cousin, Lady Jane Grey, who was a Protestant too. Lady Jane Grey's family took control of London, and the Tower, and thrust her upon the throne.

But Mary was having none of this. Schooled by her fierce mother, toughened by the difficult times she'd experienced as she was growing up, and drawing on her own immense inner strength, she roused an army in East Anglia to march on the capital. She was successful, and on 1 October 1553, she was crowned in Westminster Abbey.

This makes her – surprisingly – the only member of the Tudor dynasty to have seized the throne by force in the whole of the sixteenth century.

Queen Mary the First has a bad reputation today, mainly because as soon as she could, she restored the old Catholic religion.

Her younger sister, Elizabeth, reigning after

her, reversed that decision, and took England back in a Protestant direction. This meant that Mary, England's first ever queen, has been vilified by the Protestant historians who wrote about her reign but who didn't share her religion. Their voices were louder than those of Mary's own Catholic supporters. That's why the Protestant view of her dominates our history books, and why people call her 'Bloody Mary'.

Mary the First is often, and rightly, blamed for the deaths of many Protestants who were killed because of their religion under her regime.

But people often forget that her father and sister, Henry the Eighth and Elizabeth, also, in their turn, burned many Catholics. In sixteenth-century terms, Mary's actions weren't exceptionally cruel or unusual.

Of course, two wrongs don't make a right. But I think that today, when we live in a secular society, and it's fine to be Protestant or Catholic or whatever you want, we should perhaps try to look past the religious debates of the sixteenth century.

Perhaps we can now perceive that despite the anti-Catholic propaganda that's tarnished her image,

Mary was in fact a ruler of remarkable tenacity and strength. She showed courage, and nerve. She always sought a family, and wished to have children with her husband, Philip of Spain. It was a tragedy for her that she could not.

Mary made mistakes, but even her errors had one fortunate consequence. When her younger half-sister, Elizabeth, became queen in Mary's wake, she did such a good job that she's widely acknowledged to have been English history's most impressive sovereign.

I believe one of the reasons Queen Elizabeth the First is so widely admired is that she watched, and learned from, her sister, Mary.

Acknowledgements

My sincere thanks go to the talented Chloe Moss, who wrote the drama scenes in our television series *Six Wives with Lucy Worsley* (BBC One and PBS). A line Chloe wrote for Henry the Eighth – 'Remember what happened to my last wife!' – sparked off the idea for this story, and is included here with her generous permission. Secondly, Anna Whitelock's brilliant non-fiction history book, *Mary Tudor: England's First Queen* (Bloomsbury), argues that Mary should no longer be simply dismissed as 'bloody'. It helped me to see Mary in the new way I've shown her here. I also continue to be enormously grateful to the magnificent team I work with at Bloomsbury, particularly Helen Vick, Lizz Skelly, Charlotte Armstrong and above all editor Zöe Griffiths.

LOOK OUT FOR MORE
EXCITING HISTORICAL DRAMA
FROM LUCY WORSLEY

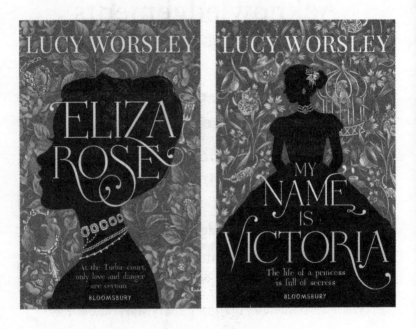